JOSHUA

THE HOMECOMING

JOSHUA

THE HOMECOMING

JOSEPH F. GIRZONE

DOUBLEDAY

New York   London   Toronto   Sydney   Auckland

PUBLISHED BY DOUBLEDAY
a division of Random House, Inc.
1540 Broadway, New York, New York 10036

DOUBLEDAY and the portrayal of an anchor with a dolphin
are trademarks of Doubleday, a division of
Random House, Inc.

Library of Congress Cataloging-in-Publication Data
Girzone, Joseph F.
Joshua, the homecoming / Joseph F. Girzone. — 1st ed.
p.   cm.
I. Title.
PS3557.I77J6   1999
813'.54—dc21   99-33129
CIP

Book design by Donna Sinisgalli
Illustrations by Stefano Vitale

ISBN 0-385-49509-9
Copyright © 1999 by Joseph F. Girzone
All Rights Reserved
Printed in the United States of America
November 1999
First Edition
1   3   5   7   9   10   8   6   4   2

There is a story behind this dedication. Sculptors see images in a raw piece of marble and chisel away at the rock
to free the image locked inside. When I was working on
the manuscript for this book, I had a difficult time finding
the hidden image. I was quite concerned, especially since
the deadline was imminent. In spite of my concern, I took
time off to attend a Christmas concert at Carnegie Hall,
sponsored by the Vatican Mission to the United Nations.
The conductor was a dear friend, Monsignor Carl Marucci.
The concert's strikingly original presentation and spirit had
a profound effect on me, flooding my mind with very moving images of Jesus. It was expressing in music just what I
was having such difficulty expressing through words in my
manuscript.

When I returned home, and continued work on the

manuscript, the story unfolded so smoothly. Finishing the manuscript then became pure joy. So, I gladly dedicate this book to my dear friend Monsignor Carl Marucci, who inspired so many of us with his moving rendition of the Christmas story.

ACKNOWLEDGMENTS

I would like to express my gratitude to Trace Murphy, my editor, and Andrew Corbin, his assistant, for their expert help in the production of this manuscript. I am also grateful to Eric Major, my publisher, for his continued reassurance at difficult moments of self-doubt, and particularly because I think he really enjoys reading my books. The publicity department has worked so hard opening new markets and introducing the books to an ever-increasing readership. To them, my special thanks. The field representatives and their colleagues I look upon as special partners, since they carry my messages far and wide, into practically every city in the country and outside the country. And what can I say about my agent, Peter Ginsberg? I see him rarely, but he has become a dear friend, as well as an excellent agent. My gratitude to him is without bounds. As I was polishing up the manuscript I became more and more impressed with the excellent and time-consuming work of the copy editor, Estelle Laurence. Her precision and dedication to every detail is remarkable. I am most grateful. I also want to thank Sister Dorothy Ederer, O.P., my partner, for her support and patience, and for her excellent advice and encouragement during difficult times. Without her help my ministry would be impossible.

JOSHUA

THE HOMECOMING

THERE ARE STORIES throughout history about mysterious appearances of the Divine Presence in people's lives. Some are mythical, and others are quite well documented, as is the case with Moses, the prophets, and many of the saints. While some people might feel God's comings and goings should be restricted as prescribed in Revelation, it seems God nonetheless still has His own mind and feels free to move about His creation as He chooses. As to the reasons for such supernatural happenings, only God can provide the answer. I like to think that as human events flow farther and farther away from the initial shock of the Resurrection, people find reasons for belief increasingly harder to accept than did people of the past. God seems to understand the difficulty of finding faith in a faithless age, and, as in the story of the Prodigal Son, condescends to our human weakness to help our unbelief. That may be the reason why Joshua, in this present story, returns for another visit, to bring comfort and hope to a people frightened about dire prophecies of imminent disaster.

It was a bitterly cold winter night. A lone stranger walked down a street in the City of Brotherly Love, not far from the old Reading Railroad Station, recently converted into the Reading Market. People were rushing—many were on their way to celebrate with friends, others to evening services, some were even last-minute shoppers, for it is Christmas Eve. The stranger was not properly dressed for such a cold night, wearing nothing more than a woolen shirt, ordinary pants, and sandals. But surprisingly enough, this man seemed unconcerned about his exposure to the elements as he stopped at the corner, looked in different directions, and began to cross the street. Seemingly out of nowhere a speeding car squealed around the corner, barely missing the stranger but managing to soak him with icy slush.

Furious at the close call, the driver yelled out the window, "Watch where you're walking, you lazy bum." Unperturbed, the stranger continued on his way as if he heard nothing, joining the people who were headed toward a church a few blocks away. No one paid much attention to the stranger, but those who did commented to their companions on how meagerly clad he was for such a freezing cold night. One lady suggested her husband give him his overcoat as he had two more at home.

"Honey, you've got to be kidding! If he wants to dress that way, that's his problem. There's no reason why he can't work like everyone else. Why should I be expected to dress him? I've never in my life ever seen a truly poor person. People like him are just too lazy to work."

The wife said nothing more and the couple hurried toward the joyful sound of Christmas hymns. Taking no notice of this exchange, the stranger himself continued toward the church. At the steps of the church, a young boy selling calendars watched with sadness as he approached.

" 'Hey, mister, you look cold. Don't you have anything better than that to wear?' "

"That's all I have, Thomas. But I don't mind."

"But you have to mind. It's a cold night. You're going to freeze, especially from that guy splashing you with slush. There he goes into the church with his family. He's not a very nice man. I know him. Here, mister, take my coat. I have a sweater underneath, so I can keep warm," the boy said as he took off his coat. It had a hole in the elbow of one sleeve. The coat was old, probably handed down in the family from one child to the next.

"By the way, mister, what's your name?"

"Joshua."

"Joshua, that's a nice name. But how did you know my name?" the boy asked, as he offered his coat to Joshua. When Joshua did not respond immediately, the boy, in his excitement to help the stranger, forgot that he never got an answer to his question.

Joshua accepted the gift so generously offered and tried

to put it on. It was clearly too small, but as he put his arm in the sleeve, it expanded to a perfect fit. As the tiny coat grew to Joshua's size, Joshua watched the boy's growing amazement and smiled. Then, taking off the coat, he gave it back to the boy. It was no longer a worn-out rag, but a beautiful new coat. The coat the boy gave Joshua, Joshua was still wearing.

"Gee, mister, how did you do that?"

Joshua smiled. "Our Father in heaven always takes good care of us, Thomas. I also noticed that people were not buying your calendars. Your Heavenly Father knows your parents need the money to buy clothes for your family for Christmas, so He blessed you. You will find what He gave you in the right hand pocket. The calendars he would like you to give to poor people when you see them tomorrow."

The boy reached into his pocket, and to his surprise, found it full of money.

The parish priest on his way to Mass watched this touching scene unfold from a distance. The boy he had known since birth. He belonged to a poor family that lived in the parish, good people struggling hard to survive. The priest had often helped them, and had allowed the boy to sell his calendars outside the church each year to earn a little money for Christmas. The priest was touched when he saw the boy offer Joshua his coat, but was awestruck at what followed. He wanted to walk over and become involved, but, out of respect for the privacy of what he was witnessing, thought it best that he wait. After Joshua gave the boy back his coat, he turned and looked over at the priest and, in a kind gesture of recognition, smiled at him. The priest then knew. He smiled and entered the church, rubbing the tears from his eyes. He turned as if he wanted to go back and talk to the stranger, but thought differently, then continued up the aisle of the church. To intrude on such an intimate encounter would be rude. It was the boy's special moment. The stranger's smile was blessing enough.

In the meantime, when the boy realized how much money there was in the pocket, he was overjoyed.

"Thank you, mister. Thank you so much. Now, I can buy my mother and father and my sisters presents for Christmas. The man at the store told me he was closing late and would wait for me, like he did last year."

"Now, go home, son, and get some sleep."

"No, no. I can't do that. I want to go in and thank Jesus. It's his birthday, you know." The boy ran up the stairs of the church and went inside. Joshua followed slowly behind, and stood there for a few moments, looking across the crowded rows of people singing the age-old songs of Jesus' birth. Their love and good will were genuine, but their understanding, like that of the people of old, was, oh, so wanting. He still loved them, and smiled at this little flock of singing sheep. He turned, walked out into the street, and continued in the direction of the Reading Market.

As Joshua walked down the street, the priest was beginning his Christmas sermon. "My dear parishioners, the sermon I had spent all week preparing, I cannot give. I have just witnessed my sermon out in front of the church. Let me tell what happened.

"You all saw that little boy outside selling calendars. His father is sickly and cannot work. The mother struggles with her five children. They have little money. I let the boy sell calendars so he can make some money to buy presents for everyone in his family; not frivolous presents, but things you and I take for granted, clothes, food, and wood to heat the house. Yes, there are people forced to live that way today. They are good people, but just down on their luck. This little boy, as young as he is, tries to help his mother.

"As I left the rectory I saw the boy standing there in the cold. He noticed a stranger without a coat and poorly dressed, walking down the street. I am sure you all also saw that stranger. The boy saw him and felt sorry for him.

" 'Mister, you look cold,' he said to him, then proceeded to take off his tiny coat with holes in it, and offer it to the stranger. The man took it, and put it on. As he did the coat began to fit him perfectly. He took off the coat that grew to size and gave it to the boy. Joshua still had on the original coat, with the holes in it. The boy could not believe his eyes, nor could I.

"Then he told the boy that God knew Thomas needed money for his family, and that only a few bought his calendars, so God bought the calendars from him, and said that he should give the calendars to poor people he would meet tomorrow. He told the boy to look in his coat pocket. When he did, he found it full of money, enough for presents for all the family.

"Then the stranger looked up at me, and smiled, as if he knew I wanted to talk to him, but that it was the boy's mo-

6

ment. But he did not have to talk to me. That knowing smile spoke to me a thousand messages, and by the look in his eyes, I knew it was God, it was Jesus who had come to visit us this evening, to share his Christmas with us. You all had a chance this evening to meet Jesus on your way into church. Did you see him? Did you smile a greeting and wish him a Merry Christmas? Were you kind to him as he walked across the street? I noticed his clothes were soaking wet. Jesus told us that we could always find him with the poor. Tonight he kept his word, and came among us as one of the poor."

The priest then bowed his head and walked back up to the altar.

In the meantime, as Joshua walked along, he approached a side street adjacent to the closed market. Walking down that street he heard music playing in the distance. He looked up a dark alley and saw the silhouettes of five figures standing around a fire under one of the massive stone arches that had been part of the railroad system of years past. The figures were playing Christmas spirituals and other carols. Walking down the alley, he saw five young men, four black men and one white man, playing guitars, flute, trumpet, and violin, as they stood around the fire.

As Joshua approached, two of the men turned and smiled a welcome. When they finished the song, they greeted the stranger, as they placed their instruments on a bench against the base of the arch.

"Hey, man, what are you doing out on a night like this?" one of the men asked.

"Just walking through the neighborhood."

"Where do you live?"

"No place in particular. I just wander around from place to place."

"Come over closer to the fire! Hey, what happened to you, man? Your clothes are soaked! You must be freezing! Stand here next to the fire and dry off so you don't catch pneumonia."

One of the men, a thin, powerfully built black man in his late twenties, with a goatee, picked up a bowl and asked Joshua if he would like a bowl of soup.

"It will at least warm your insides, so you don't freeze."

"I sure would appreciate a bowl of hot soup. Thank you, Hakim," Joshua said.

"How'd you know my name?"

"I've known all of you all your lives," Joshua answered.

"How do you know us? I never saw you before."

"I know you and have watched over you. You have gone through very difficult times, but have kept your spirit. You are good young men, and you have brought strength to many people. Your music has comforted more troubled people than you could ever imagine. Don't lose your happy spirit, no matter how difficult times may be. The way you live now, as painful and lonely as it is, is the way Jesus once lived, with no place to lay his head and no warm bed to sleep in. But by his life he brought God's love to the world. You bring God's love in a different way, by the example of your goodness and the happy spirit of your music."

"You give me goose bumps the way you talk. But thanks for all the nice things you say. Now how about some of that soup? There's plenty to go around."

"Thank you."

Over the fire was a grill about four feet square. In the middle was a pot of soup. Thanking him, Joshua took a few sips of the chicken broth.

"Besides everything else, you are good cooks," Joshua said.

"When we have something to cook," one man said, to everyone's laughter.

"Yeah, we're just lucky tonight," one fellow said. "The Italian butcher down the street knows us since we were kids, and every now and then gives us enough to last for a few days. Tonight we have a feast."

"Thank you for sharing it. You will never be hungry again," Joshua said. But his tone was so nonchalant it made no impression.

"Wouldn't that be great, if we could eat every day?" the white man added.

When he finished the soup, Joshua thanked the men and started to leave.

"Where're you going? You haven't heard our concert yet. We were just getting warmed up before you came. In fact, you're welcome to stay with us tonight and sleep near the hot fire. It's not too bad when there's no wind."

"You are very kind and generous," Joshua replied. "I would be happy to stay."

So, after singing carols and hymns, and exchanging stories, the six men lay down around the fire, and covered with old blankets, they fell asleep under the stars that cold winter night. It was only after Joshua left the next morning that the men realized who it was who had stayed with them that blessed evening. They were shocked to find that boxes and boxes of all sorts of food surrounded them—steaks, fruit, bread, wine. And the pot of soup was still full, and would continue to be full for a long time to come, until someone was kind enough to hire the men, giving them decent jobs.

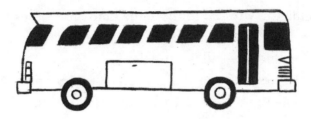

IT WAS THE evening of Christmas Day when Joshua turned up many miles away in a village he had visited years before. Walking down the side street amid the falling snow, Joshua knocked at the front door of the house of Pat and Minnie Zumbar. Many of the old friends had died, and Pat, who reminded Joshua of Peter of long ago, would certainly welcome him to their home, even at that late hour of the night.

Pat almost fainted when he opened the door and saw Joshua standing there in the cold. "I thought you were dead. What are you doing wandering around on a bitter cold night like this?"

Hearing her husband's loud voice, Minnie could not believe her ears. "Joshua?" she yelled out in shock. "Well, bring him inside, you darn fool. Don't let him just stand out there freezing."

"Come on in, Joshua," Pat said apologetically. "I was so shocked to see you, I was beside myself. Come on in and warm up. You must be freezing! Don't you have any winter clothes? I guess you never had to wear winter clothes where you come from. Mine certainly won't fit you, but tomorrow we can find some."

Joshua was dressed in the same kinds of clothes Pat had last seen him wearing, except now he had the old coat with holes in it, and was still in sandals.

As Pat and Minnie did not take strong drink, Minnie prepared a cup of hot tea with lemon for Joshua, while Pat got some things from the refrigerator. "Joshua, we have the leftovers of the chicken dinner we had for supper. Would that be all right?"

"Please don't fuss. I really don't have to have anything."

Pat put the dish of chicken, potatoes, and green beans in the oven, and while waiting for them to heat up, sat down at the table and started to ply Joshua with a thousand questions.

"You know, you're quite a mystery. What happened to you after you went to Rome? Someone said you just vanished into thin air."

Joshua laughed. It was a full, hearty laugh as if he was delighted that his disappearance had generated such curiosity.

"When my work was finished I left," Joshua said without any further explanation.

Seeing that Joshua did not intend to tell any more, Pat let the matter drop.

"What brings you back to town now?" Pat asked.

"Why don't you leave the poor man alone?" Minnie interjected. "He just drops in to visit and you grill him like the district attorney."

"Joshua"—she turned to their visitor—"do you like your tea plain or with sugar and lemon, or how do you like it?"

"With lemon and a little sugar will be fine."

"I know you'd probably prefer a glass of wine and it would be good on a cold night like this, but Pat and I don't drink, so we rarely have it in the house."

"The hot tea is just fine."

Minnie proceeded to pour the tea for the three of them, then, sitting down at the table, became part of the conversation.

"We really missed you after you left last time," Minnie said. "What happened in Rome? Were they nice to you?"

"It was businesslike. I went because I had messages to deliver. I was deeply troubled by some of the things I experienced there. Shepherds should always treat the sheep with respect. But it was good to see Peter. He has a difficult task, but he is carrying out his responsibilities well. He is a dedicated shepherd. He's faithful, he's sincere, and he cares. He teaches what is good in season and out of season without regard for society's changing moral fashions. He is truly the Rock Jesus intended. His strength and single-mindedness were needed for the times. The shepherd who follows him will show another side and will heal many wounds. He will bring the sheep of different flocks closer to Jesus' prayer that there be 'one flock and one shepherd.' "

"Joshua, Minnie and I feel honored you came to visit us. Can you stay with us? We would love to have you. It is cold outside and the old house you used to live in is occupied."

"I was hoping you would take me in. It is too cold to stay outside. It is not like the days of old when one could sleep out in the hills. The weather there was more hospitable."

"Joshua, we know who you are so you don't have to put on a big front anymore," Pat blurted out.

Horrified at Pat's bluntness, Minnie shot back at him, "I can't believe you said that, Pat."

Then, turning to Joshua, "I'm sorry about my husband's rudeness, Joshua. He has such a big mouth."

Joshua laughed. "That's why I like him, Minnie, and why I feel comfortable with him. He is just himself. He's real. He's a lot like Peter in the old days. He's even built like him, like a little bull, almost as wide as he is tall. You need not feel embarrassed over him. He has a kind heart."

"See, Minnie, he understands me," Pat said. "Well, I'll still call you Joshua even though I know your real name, because Joshua is the name you originally told us. And I promise to keep it to ourselves. But I would like to call the whole gang together and have a party. We're still celebrating your birthday, you know."

"I wasn't really born on December twenty-fifth. It's just a day a monk picked a long time ago to celebrate my coming into this world to coincide with the increasing daylight."

"I know. The priest told us at church the other day. But

one day's as good as another, especially since you don't let anybody know anything about yourself, including the date you were born."

Joshua laughed and said nothing.

"Well, it's late," Minnie interjected, "and Joshua looks like he needs a good sleep. So, I'll get his bed ready."

The next morning, Joshua was the first one up. It was still snowing. The early morning sun was bright, and Joshua delighted at the sight of three youngsters playing in the snow. He quietly slipped out the front door and walked slowly toward the children, a little girl about five, and two boys, no more than five or six. They had snowballs in their hands and were about to throw them at a passing bakery truck when they spotted Joshua. As he approached they looked frightened, until he spoke to them.

"Good morning!" he said to them.

They looked at him strangely. They had never seen him before. They knew Pat and Minnie, but who was this man coming out of their house? His summer clothes and sandals made them wonder even more.

"Don't be afraid, I am a friend of Pat and Minnie. The last time I visited them you were not even born yet. I know my clothes and sandals look funny in this kind of weather, but it is all I have. Besides, the cold weather doesn't bother me very much."

The children relaxed at the man's friendliness and asked him his name.

"My name is Joshua."

"Oh, I know you," the girl said. "My parents talk about you a lot. And my grandparents do, too."

"So do ours," the boys chimed in. "You're famous."

"What are *your* names?" Joshua asked.

"Mine is Joan."

"Mine is Mike."

"And mine is Tony. Would you like to play snowballs with us?"

"How do you play that?"

"Well, when a truck comes by, we throw snowballs at it. It's easy. Sometimes the drivers get mad at us, so we run."

"Well, I don't think that would be good for my reputation, throwing snowballs at passing trucks. People get mad at me enough when things don't go their way, without them getting mad at me for throwing snowballs at them. Why don't we invent a new game where no one gets hurt? It will be fun."

"Okay, what is it?" Mike asked.

"Suppose we call it just 'Make Believe!' "

"How does it go?" Tony asked.

"Like this. See that tire over there hanging from the tree?"

"Yes, what about it?" Mike said.

"Take turns trying to throw snowballs through the tire. Make believe you're a baseball pitcher and the tire is the batter. See how many batters you can strike out. Then, when you get really good at it, you can swing the tire back and forth, and try throwing the snowballs through it."

"What about me? I can't throw snowballs like that," Joan complained.

"I've got something special for you, Joan. Make square snowballs like this one. Then make a checkerboard with them on the driveway here that no one uses. After you make your checkerboard, try to jump between the snow blocks. See how many you can jump over before you miss and kick one. It's like snow hopscotch. If you get from one side to the other without knocking over any blocks you win, you get a point. You watch, the boys will give up their make-believe baseball and want to beat you at jumping over the blocks."

Before long the children were engrossed in their games. Joshua helped the boys get their game started, then started Joan on making her snow blocks, and showed her how to hopscotch over them. When the little girl tried it, she was really good at it, and after a few tries was able to jump over them all without kicking over any of the blocks. Just as Joshua predicted, the boys came over and wanted to play Joan's game, to see if they could beat her at it.

While the children were engrossed in the game, Joshua left and walked back to Pat and Minnie's house. He knew Minnie was hard at work preparing breakfast; the aroma of bacon sizzling in the pan floated through the open window into the brisk, cold air.

Joshua walked into the house and was immediately confronted by Pat. "Where did you go so early in the morning?"

"I just took a walk down the street, and stopped to play in the snow with three delightful children."

"You must be freezing. It's cold out there. The weatherman said it's twenty degrees! Weren't you cold?"

"I didn't notice it, I was having so much fun with the children."

"You're a strange man, Joshua. We'll have to get you some warm clothes so you don't freeze to death."

During breakfast, Pat had a thousand questions like, "What are you doing back here now? Are you going to give us a preview of the Second Coming? Are you happy with what you see in the world, and in the Church?"

Joshua just smiled and said, "There is still work to be done. It's a long time since the Resurrection. Events once so clear and dramatic have faded with the passing of time. My disciples should have kept my life alive to the hurting peoples of the world, but they have failed to reflect my life to others, because they have not understood me. Now it is difficult to tell the difference between a Christian and an atheist. In fact, there are many atheists and Jews who reflect my love and my spirit more faithfully than do my disciples. In Christian countries there is so much greed and hatred and poverty. Forgiveness is a virtue long forgotten among Christians. They have become known for their vindictiveness. In the days of Rome, the emperors would order the soldiers to throw Christians to the lions. Now it could be said about people whom you don't like, 'Throw them to the Christians.' It is a sad commentary on what has happened to my people. You see it in political witch-hunts as self-righteous Christians 'assassinate' opponents, and drag people's private lives before the world, as the Pharisees did to the woman they caught in adultery. When pagan people witness this, why would they want to follow me? Religion appears to them to be just a sham, and I see today what I found so distasteful in religion of old, scribes and Pharisees in love with religion and its endless laws and prohibitions, but insensitive to the love of God and the pain and suffering in people's lives. Oh, I know there are many good people, as there were good scribes and Pharisees in days gone by. But they are so few by comparison to the many who hurt and wound the flock by their obsession with laws and prohibitions. People now have a difficult time finding me in many churches. As a result, I am no longer real, just a historical figure who has little effect on the life of the Church and on the minds of church leaders. Finely chiseled laws and concepts, and quoting chapter and verse of scripture, have taken the place of the living Jesus, who shared divine relationships and a beautiful way of living. Perhaps the work my Father gave me is still unfinished because my disciples have failed to carry on the Good News as I intended."

"Are things really that bad, Joshua? I know we certainly are not ideal, but you speak as if things seem almost hopeless."

"No, never hopeless, and we can never become discouraged. But when you see things through God's heart, you cannot help but be distressed at the injustice and meanness in the world, especially among those who should reflect God's goodness."

"Why doesn't God do something about it?" Pat questioned.

"Because He respects the free will He gave to people. Even when they abuse it He cannot take away people's freedom, just as He cannot stop loving people when they do evil. God's goodness is not determined by people's actions. His love is irrevocable. God is very patient. People want immediate results. God's justice is much more thorough than human justice. Those who suffer injustice now will be rewarded in ways the human mind could never believe, and those who are cruel and unjust now will suffer pain from guilt that will be too hard to bear and live."

"Pat, will you stop asking Joshua such heavy questions for breakfast! We're all going to get indigestion. Give him a rest, will you?"

"Minnie, give me a break! He likes to answer questions like that."

Joshua just smiled and continued eating his breakfast.

When they had finished eating, Pat helped Minnie clean up. Joshua was impressed and even offered to help. Minnie acted offended, so he just stood around and talked.

After cleaning up, Pat went to the phone to tell what was left of the old gang that Joshua was back. They didn't even wait for an invitation. They just ran over to Pat and Minnie's and made themselves at home. Joshua was happy that they felt so comfortable with him. It was what he had always wanted people to feel about him.

There weren't too many of the old gang left. Those who were still alive were fifteen years older. Some limped into the house. Others had to be helped. All had aches they never knew existed. But they were still their old happy, genial selves, full of good spirits and mischief.

Joe Langford came. He was the one whose farm and flock of sheep bordered on Joshua's old cottage. His wife Mary had died and Joe's life had never been the same, especially since so many of his friends had also gone home to God. Jimmy Dicara had died. His parting was a loss to everyone, as they looked to him for wisdom and a cool head in difficult times. Moe Sanders was gone, but his wife, Mary, and Moe's brothers, Freddie and George, and his wife,

Katherine, were there. Anne, Mary's friend from the diner, came. Long John had died, as had Herm Ianutti, but Long John's wife, Dolores, came. John the mailman arrived with Henry Persini. Everyone missed Henry's brother Ernie, who had recently passed away.

They were at first curious at seeing Joshua. So many rumors had spread through the neighborhood since his previous departure, they didn't know what to expect. But within a few minutes, they realized nothing had changed. Joshua was the same natural, relaxed Joshua—acting as if nothing had happened and as if all those years had not passed.

Before long, they were engrossed in heavy conversation, with everyone talking and, as usual, no one listening. Minnie, like a good Martha, was busy about many things, principally, making sure the snack dishes were full and placed at strategic places around the house. Like Pat had been, everyone was curious about what happened to Joshua after he left last time. He shared some of the happenings, but as he was not the type to share things personal between himself and others, he was discreet in his answers. He told them few details of his experiences in Rome, but did say that, overall, his visit was not unpleasant.

They couldn't wait to tell him that their old pastor was gone, and that they had a new one. Joshua's only concern was whether the Holy Spirit was really welcome in the community and "allowed" to freely function in the lives of the people. Part of that concern was whether the people were allowed to obey the promptings of the Spirit, or to do what the pastor told them they could do, which was often enough nothing.

The party broke up before noon, as people had things scheduled for the day. But Joshua was invited to each of their homes—invitations which he graciously accepted. As they were leaving, the subject of Father Pat came up. Freddie asked if Joshua had heard about him since he left the parish. Joshua did not let on he knew anything, but listened intently. Freddie went on to say how Father Pat took a leave of absence to go to school, like a sabbatical. When he came back, he told the bishop he no longer wanted to do parish work, but insisted on bringing the gospel message to people who did not as yet know Jesus. He thought Jesus never intended that priests stay in parishes and save the same souls over and over, week after week. That seemed to Father Pat a form of benign and comfortable servitude. But because Father Pat was a good priest, the bishop was not willing to lose him and so he let him form an evangelizing team. Pat and his team now went from place to place, sometimes to malls, sometimes to parties people arranged in their homes, sometimes to churches, Protestant and Catholic, sometimes even to synagogues. People liked him a lot, so he got invited everywhere.

"But you always knew he was a good priest, didn't you, Joshua? Everyone could tell by the way you were with him," Freddie said.

"Yes, Pat was always a good priest. He was wonderfully human and did not hide his frailty, which never detracted from his goodness. He is a good shepherd. There should be many more like him."

"It didn't bother you that he had a drinking problem?" Freddie asked.

"No," Joshua said with a laugh. "Everyone has a problem of some sort or other. People just have to make the best of their weaknesses. In time they will outgrow them if they work at it. It is their frailty that draws forth God's compassion. It's the ones who look upon themselves as righteous, whom everyone else should imitate, that God has a problem with. They lack compassion and belittle those they consider sinners. Their arrogance is an insurmountable barrier to God."

"Those are tough words, Joshua," Pat said.

"It is not that God is tough, but when people are cruel and condemning, they push God away from them. When He reaches out to them, they turn the other way. They resent a compassionate, forgiving God. They demand a God who will inflict severe punishment on sinners. My Father is not a punishing God. He is a God of love. In the judgment, people judge themselves; when they see infinite love in my Father's eyes they know whether they are worthy to live in His Presence."

"Pat, will you leave the poor man alone," Minnie complained. "He's probably exhausted with all the fellows fussing over him."

"Joshua, I apologize. Why don't you take a rest while I go out and get some presentable clothes for you to wear."

While Joshua rested, the weather took a turn for the worse. A storm from the west dropped another eight inches of snow on the eighteen already covering the ground. The snow muffled Pat's footsteps as he came up the stairs, but his voluminous voice shattered the peace that had settled over the place when he left.

"Well, I'm home. Wait till you see what I got, you guys," he called out as he came through the door.

The noise woke Minnie out of a deep sleep. She looked up from the couch where she had been lying, got up, and opened the packages her husband brought over to her. Even she was surprised at the good taste Pat had shown in picking out clothes for Joshua.

"These are really nice, Pat," she commented. "They fit Joshua's personality perfectly. He's going to look real sharp in these things."

As she was speaking, Joshua emerged from the bedroom, looking sleepy-eyed.

"Well, while you guys were resting, I was working hard. Look what I picked up, Joshua."

Joshua was wide-eyed at the clothes Pat bought for him. Even he was surprised at Pat's good taste. "Pat, you went out and bought new clothes. That was not necessary, but I am grateful."

"Try them on. I hope you like them."

Joshua changed into the new clothes and he looked proud indeed. Even he felt good in them.

"It is amazing what a new set of clothes can do for a person," Joshua said, on emerging from the bedroom all dressed up. Pat and Minnie couldn't tell by the broad grin on his face whether he was making fun of the way people talk when they get new clothes or whether he really did feel good about the way he looked. The light brown pants weren't much different from the khaki he had been wearing, maybe a shade or two darker, but with the yellow shirt, he really looked sharp. The shoes were the kind you could wear in the snow, with thick soft rubber bottoms. Pat swelled with pride when he looked at him, and could tell by the look on Joshua's face that he was really pleased.

"Put on the coat, Joshua! See how it fits!" Pat said.

The coat was of waterproof microfiber material that could be worn in any kind of weather. It fit perfectly. Joshua cut a handsome figure in his new outfit.

"Now, I know you didn't come just to visit us. So, the next question is where do you go from here?" Pat said brusquely.

Joshua laughed at Pat's perceptiveness.

"My mission has no end as my Father's work is never finished. His love is forever creative," Joshua replied rather casually.

"That's some statement, Joshua. Does that mean the world will never come to an end?" Pat asked with an impish look.

Joshua smiled. He was not upset. "There is no end to creation, just transition from one form to another."

"You mean the world will last forever?" Pat asked.

"The world as people know it will change, but the change will be gradual and gentle, nothing that will terrorize people. My Father does nothing violently. Only people's interference can bring about violent change."

"What about all the prophecies? They tell of terrible things that are going to happen."

"Pat, my Father is not a monster. He does not do terrible things. It is people's fears that create nightmares out of scripture and imagine things that will never take place. Why would my Father want to strike terror into his children's

hearts? It doesn't make sense. He is a God of love and compassion. He created the universe with immense thought and
love, so His children could enjoy what He gave them. He is
not a God who enjoys terrorizing people."

"But in the Book of Revelation . . ."

"Many of the events in Revelation have already taken
place. Those prophecies deal with things that happened in
days of old, and with circumstances surrounding the destruction of life as they knew it. It was not my Father's doing. Some of the events in that book hint of things to come,
but if evil things happen, it will be the work of human beings, not the work of my Father. My Father does not do evil
things to His children. He cares for them with tenderness."

"Then you don't think we should be afraid of the world
coming to an end?" Minnie interjected.

"Dear Minnie, God does not play games. Why would
God bring the world to a sudden end? The world ends for
each one when he or she dies. That is the only end that people should be concerned about. The rest is beyond human
comprehension. When and if the world ends, most creatures
will not be around to see it. Humanity is not an experiment
by God. It is an ongoing expression of my Father's love,
which will not come to an abrupt end. People may end life
on earth by themselves if they do not care for the world my
Father gave them, but my Father's love for humanity will not
end until His creation is perfected. That will only happen
when all humanity is transformed into a faithful image of
God's Son, and is presented to the Father by the Son. Only
then will the Savior's work be totally complete. So, you see

there is still much work to be done, work which will take a long, long time."

"What about the great battle between good and evil at the end of time?" Minnie continued.

"That battle is waged daily. If you could see the spirit world, you would see continual conflict between good and evil. Every person is involved each day in that battle. Their spirit friends are by their side in those daily struggles, just as evil persons try to seduce them into evil ways. In the end that battle will merely become visible, and the powers from heaven will reach down to call the faithful home. Don't get caught up in the nightmares conjured up by false prophets to frighten and terrorize. Remember Jesus has set you free. Do not fall back into enslavement to fear and guilt."

"I know you're not planning on staying with us, Joshua. What do you intend to do next?"

"Pat, I will leave tomorrow. These are troubled times and people live on the edge of panic. I will be where I am needed. Pray constantly, but pray with love and not fear. Your prayers should be gentle conversations with your Father. In that intimacy you will find comfort and strength."

The rest of the day went by fast, too fast, as far as Minnie and Pat were concerned. They wanted Joshua never to leave. They felt such reassurance from his presence—if only he could stay longer.

Tomorrow did come too soon. When Joshua walked out into the snow the next day, Minnie and Pat watched him as he disappeared down the street. He was a lonely figure seemingly walking out into nowhere, through the falling snow. Where would he go on a day like that? Who would ever know him, much less welcome him as he, unfamiliar to everyone, strolled into a strange neighborhood? The couple held each other's hands as they walked back into their warm house, a tear in their eyes and a sad feeling in their hearts. The house suddenly seemed so empty.

When the others heard that Joshua had already left their neighborhood, they felt an extraordinary sadness, a loneliness they could not understand. In talking to one another, they realized they all shared a feeling of loss they had never experienced about anyone else. It was almost as if a part of their very self was missing.

Minnie had surreptitiously slipped a few hundred dollars into Joshua's coat pocket before he left. She knew he would need it. And he did. He used part of it for bus fare to get where he intended to go. No one knew him at the little bus stop on the main street. Part novelty store, part grocery store, it served as the city's bus terminal. Joshua went inside, where two or three others were waiting for the bus to arrive.

When the bus came, it was not even half full. Joshua took a seat toward the back on the right side, where he could look out the window. It is a melancholy feeling riding on a bus in the wintertime, as the snow is falling. You feel an odd kind of emptiness, as if you are really alone in the world, and belong to no one. I could understand Joshua's feelings, because that was the way I felt when I traveled by bus as a young teenager going back to the seminary after Christmas vacation. I felt terribly alone.

At the next city, Joshua changed buses and boarded one that was going up into the mountains. The scenery outside the city was breathtaking. The snow was pure white, brilliant in the bright sun, like a million sparkling diamonds. Joshua looked out the window, deep in thought, enjoying the feelings of nostalgia that you experience only in circumstances like this.

As the bus left the populated areas, the countryside opened up like a winter wonderland. In one backyard a man was chopping thick logs in half and stacking them into a neat pile while a little boy looked on. Joshua smiled as he remembered watching his father busy at work. It seemed like yesterday. In another backyard, a woman was taking clothes off a line. They were frozen stiff, and she piled a few at a time on the back porch. Her pet dog snatched one off the pile and ran out into the deep snow with the woman screaming after him.

The bus wound its way down toward the river road as it turned north. A lonely oil barge floated lazily through the partially frozen water. A lone sailor walked along the deck, smoking a cigarette as he watched the snow falling on the icy river. Joshua could sense his turmoil and murmured a silent blessing for the man. Life on the Sea of Galilee was paradise compared to boat life in frigid weather.

The drone of the bus's engine lulled Joshua into a deep sleep. When he woke it was well past noon, and he realized he was not far from his destination up in the mountains. Besides Joshua, only two passengers were left, a middle-aged woman and a young boy no more than eight. As the bus approached the old-fashioned mountain village, the boy sprang to life. "Mama, Mama, look at the horse and sleigh! Is that Santa Claus' sleigh?"

The boy had obviously never seen a horse-drawn sleigh before, except in pictures of Santa Claus with his reindeers.

"No, son, that's the way some people live way up here in the mountains. They like to live the way people lived years ago. We are going to be living like that soon."

"You mean we are going to have a horse and sleigh like that?" the boy asked with an awed expression.

"Perhaps. Where we are going is different from living at home. We have to be totally dependent on ourselves for survival, so we have to learn how to live without all the things we're used to."

"That's going to be fun," the boy said, without realizing all the boring chores he would end up with.

Joshua listened with interest.

The bus stop was a small antique building, the kind one would see in a Dickens movie. A small group stood on the sidewalk waiting for the bus to arrive.

"You're Melanie?" a middle-aged woman asked the lady just alighting from the bus with her son.

"Yes, and this is my son, Jonathan. Say hello to the people, Jonathan."

"Melanie, my name is Sarah, and these are your new friends," the woman continued, as she introduced each one.

Jonathan kept watching the horse and sleigh, hoping that they would be riding in that.

"Jonathan, do you like the sleigh?" one of the men asked.

"Yes, I love it. Is it yours?"

"Well, yes, it really belongs to our group, our family of friends. There is another one behind the building. You can ride in this one if you like. The women like to ride together. They usually have so much to talk about as they get acquainted."

Joshua watched and listened intently, curious about these people who were embarking on a new life totally different from the life they had been living. He knew he would be seeing more of these people in the days to come.

The little party climbed into their sleighs, bundled up in the heavy blankets, and pulled the reins for the horses to take off on their trip far up into the mountains.

Joshua had only a small duffel bag with all his belongings. As he walked along the sidewalk, a frail old man was crossing the street, lighting an antique hand-carved pipe while he shuffled along. A truck had just turned the corner and slid on the icy surface as it emerged from the turn, heading straight for the old man. Joshua quickly dropped the duffel bag and ran toward him, grabbing him by the arm and pulling him out of the way of the oncoming truck.

The stunned man, thinking he was being assaulted, cried out for help. But when he realized what was happening, he apologized, picked up his pipe from the snow, and thanked Joshua profusely.

"Son, I am grateful to you. I had no idea what was going on. I am sorry for being so rude."

"You weren't rude," Joshua said, "just frightened. I'm glad nothing happened to your pipe. That is a fine piece of craftsmanship."

"Thank you. This pipe was given to me many years ago

by an old woodsman, who was really a hermit, lived up in these parts all his life. Took a liking to me, I guess. I used to visit him when I was a young man. He taught me a lot about living in the wilderness. I thought he was lonely, but as I got to know him, I began to realize he wasn't lonely. He was just sick of people. He was a simple man, and couldn't understand people's complicated ways. He felt people were basically not honest, so he decided to live by himself and had as little to do as possible with people. By the way, what's your name, son? My name is Allen, Allen Danby."

"My name is Joshua. Pleased to meet you, Allen."

"Not half as pleased as I am to meet you. I wouldn't be here now if you hadn't come along. Where you staying, son?"

"No place really. I just came to town."

"Have family here?"

"No. Just came to see what life is like up this way."

"Well, you're welcome to stay at my place, seeing I owe my life to you. I have no family here either. All dead, I guess. Had a few brothers but they thought I was odd, so they never bothered with me. Took a long time getting used to, but I learned to make do with whatever life brings along. I'm stopping here in the store for a minute. Have to pick up some tobacco. It'll take just a minute, then I'll take you home with me if you like. I think you'll find it comfortable enough. Couple extra rooms, so you can be on your own, and have some privacy. You won't have to be bored by an old man like me."

"You're a real *gentle* man, Allen. I am very grateful to

you for your hospitality. I really had no place to stay to-night."

"God always provides, son. I learned a long time ago to trust Him. Had to, there was nobody else who cared. My mother died when I was young. My father favored my brothers because they were like him, interested in business deals and making money. I was a dreamer, I guess. I don't know what I was. Just different maybe. But I had to make do on my own. God became a good friend, about my only friend."

After buying tobacco, the two emerged from the store, then walked down the street, up a side street, then through a grove of trees into a little clearing. At the opposite side of the clearing stood a small house, a quaint picturesque home surrounded by a white picket fence recently painted.

"That's my house there, son. Built it with my own hands over forty years ago. Got the plans from a book in the library and little by little put it all together."

"It's a beautiful house. You are very talented, Allen."

"Thank you. I like to do things with my hands. I like to help people. Well, here we are. You go inside first. I'll make sure the door closes tight behind us so the wind doesn't come through. Gets mighty cold these nights."

"It's nice and warm in here, Allen. Do you have a furnace?"

"No, just my faithful ol' wood-burning stove out in the kitchen. Real old. Air-tight. Uses only a few logs a day and a few more at night. Keeps the place toasty warm even on the coldest days. You can see I have a fireplace in here, mostly for atmosphere, but it keeps the living room comfortable."

The old man took off his coat and hung it on a hook on the back of the door.

"You can put your coat there on the hook next to mine, Joshua," he said.

"Thanks, Allen," Joshua said as he removed his coat and hung it next to the old man's.

"I am just about to have supper, young man. Would you join me?"

"I would be honored. Thank you."

The old man uncovered a pan. The odor of simmering stew filled the room, making Joshua's mouth water.

"Smells good," Joshua said. "You seem to be quite a cook."

"You learn a lot when you live alone. I like to cook. For me it is a form of art, and takes up a good part of my day. It's been lonely lately. Not many friends left. New people in town avoid me. Think I'm odd. I guess we all seem odd when we get old. Guess I probably am odd. You get that way living by yourself for so long."

"Your life has been a good one, Allen. You are not odd. You are one of the few people who have kept their pride in being just yourself. Being different is not being odd. It is being special, the way God created you, one of a kind. And you certainly are one of a kind."

The old man looked up at Joshua to see if he was smiling. He was. The old man also smiled, his lips curling in a wry, knowing grin. He knew he was odd. Joshua was kind in making him feel special. He was that, too, Joshua was telling him.

Opening the oven door, the old man reached in and

pulled out of the hot oven two round loaves of thick-crusted bread. The oven was attached to the stove as one unit, so the oven was always hot when a fire was burning in the stove. It made for a fine even heat, and perfectly baked bread.

Joshua watched Allen as he put the bread on top of the oven. His hard, callused hands seemed insensitive to the scorching hot crust.

"Sit down, young man! Make yourself at home! I'll be ready in a minute. Soon as I get this stew dished out. Like stew, Joshua?"

"Don't remember having stew before, Allen. Smells delicious. I'm sure I'll devour it."

"It's a recipe my mother gave me when I was a little boy. She was sick one day, sick in bed, she was, and couldn't cook for the family. So, when I came home from school, she asked me if I would help her. I felt sorry for my mom. She was sick a lot. She taught me from her bed how to cook. Simple things usually. I think she sort of knew I would always be alone. It was her way of preparing me to care for myself. The recipes were easy, but good-tasting, things she knew I would be able to cook without much fuss. Good woman, my mom. Think of her a lot now that I'm old. Guess I'll be seeing her soon. Hope so anyway."

As the man rattled on, Joshua listened attentively. A lot flowed from the old man's heart. Joshua felt his pain, the pain of a lifelong loneliness. It was not by accident that Joshua met him as he exited the bus in the village. Joshua's chance encounters were never accidental. Though Joshua's life seemed on the surface casual and carefree, every moment was precisely ordered, and encounters were never haphazard. It was his genius that made it appear so simple and unplanned.

Joshua enjoyed watching the old man. His movements were measured and economical. Joshua could tell he was accustomed to following the same routine day after day. It gives security to the elderly to do the same things each day, and in exactly the same way.

Taking one of the loaves of bread and the knife lying on the table, Allen cut four thick slices. "Joshua, if you want more, feel free to cut it for yourself."

Then dishing out the stew in two big bowls, he placed one in front of his guest. It was steaming hot. "I hope you don't mind, son, but I don't drink strong drink anymore, so I don't have any in the house. I just drink water now. I do have tea and cocoa if you like."

"A glass of water will be fine, Allen. I'm just fortunate you invited me over for dinner."

The old man sat down, and bowed his head. "Lord, thank you for this nice stranger coming to visit me. Bless our food, too, Lord. And be a light to guide Joshua on his way. Thank you, God. Amen." If the man only knew who had visited him, and was sitting at his table!

"I suppose you noticed the horses and sleighs when you got off the bus, Joshua?"

"Yes, I was surprised that people still use them."

"Not many. They used to be common around here years ago. But I haven't seen one in fifty years, until the new people who moved into town last year. They use them. Don't believe in modern things. Simple people, I guess. People call *them* odd, too. Even seem odd to me. They live up in the hills, six or seven miles out. About four, five hundred of them now. They live off the land, and store things in a deep cave where the food will keep. There's a preacher who keeps them in tow, got them all in his power. He thinks the End Times are coming sometime soon and all kinds of bad things are going to happen. He has the people scared half out of their skins. But they listen to him and obey whatever he tells them. It doesn't make much sense to me. I've seen a lot of these people in my lifetime. Every so often a group like that springs up, think the world's coming to an end. They get caught up in it for a while, then, when nothing happens, they drift apart and disappear."

"I watched these people when I got off the bus," Joshua said. "They seem like good people, just terribly frightened. It is easy for preachers to take advantage of simple people like that. Those kinds of preachers may know their Bible, but they do not know God. In not knowing God, they fail to understand His Word."

"This group seems harmless enough," Allen said. "Their minister is a fellow by the name of Miller, Bobby Joe Miller. His followers come from all over. He must have recruiters, because every day people come from around the country, people of different ages. Rather simple as you say, and just looking for someone to show them a shortcut to salvation. The way I see it, there ain't no shortcut. You work it out over a lifetime. Hard work, too. 'Full time job,' my mom used to say."

"You're a good cook, Allen. The stew is delicious. You also make a good bread, good strong wheat, the kind the Roman soldiers used to eat when on the march."

"Thank you, son. I like to cook. Bake bread two, three times a week. Eat simple most of the time. Where you from, if you don't mind my asking?"

"I travel from place to place. I like to travel. It gives me a chance to visit different places, see the beautiful sights, meet people and learn their ways."

"You certainly came at an unwelcome time. Gets cold here, and snows practically every day. I hope you got warm clothes, young man. The weather's mean around these parts. And the wind is merciless."

"I can handle it. The cold doesn't bother me. Hot summers are harder to bear."

When they had finished supper, Joshua picked up what few dishes there were and brought them to the sink. As he washed them, the old man brushed the crumbs from the table, and damped the fire to cool the house for the night.

"Healthier sleeping in a cool house, Joshua. I didn't turn it down too much, just enough to sleep comfortable."

"That's fine."

"Not much doing here at night. I don't have a TV, and not much on the radio up here, so I retire early and get up early. I'll show you to your bedroom."

The old man brought Joshua around the stove to the opposite side of the house. The bedroom was quite large, nicely furnished with what seemed to be homemade furniture, carefully crafted.

"The furniture is exquisite," Joshua said. "I can tell it was made by a master."

"You are a diplomat, Joshua. How did you know I made it myself?"

"I see your personality in every line and curve, very careful workmanship. You must be proud of it."

"I am. It took a lot of time, since I learned as I went along, but with patience and persistence, I finally finished each piece. I don't do it anymore. Don't have the energy. I'll leave you to yourself now. Wake up when you want. I wake early and walk to the village to see some of my old friends. Not many left now, so we get together to see who survived the night. Every now and then somebody's missing. Makes us all sad, and feel very fragile. But we have a happy spirit and have fun, what few we are left. If you'd like to come with me, I think you'd enjoy meeting my old cronies."

"Sounds like fun. I'll be up in plenty of time. Good night, and thank you for your hospitality, Allen."

CHAPTER 3

THE NEXT MORNING was a winter wonderland, with almost a foot of snow fallen silently overnight. Joshua was the first one up and quietly slipped outside and shoveled the walk. Hearing the shovel scraping along the pavement, the old man awoke, peeked out the window, and was deeply moved to see this stranger shoveling his sidewalk.

Hurrying downstairs, he opened the front door yelling, "Young man, you don't have to do that. Come inside here; it is cold out there."

Joshua looked up, smiled, and replied, "I don't get a chance to do this every day. It is fun. Besides, I am almost finished anyway. It's a good way to work up an appetite for breakfast."

"Well, you're certainly going to need your appetite.

When you finish we'll go down to the village and have a real lumberjack's breakfast."

The village restaurant was quiet. Only three or four of Allen's friends had arrived. The rest were still plowing driveways and shoveling sidewalks.

"What will it be, gentlemen?" the cook said, as he put cups of steaming coffee in front of the two men.

"Hot cakes and sausages, Max," Allen shot back.

"And your friend? What will he have?" the cook asked, then looked straight at Joshua.

"I'll have the same thing. If Allen likes it, it has to be good. He's quite a chef, you know."

"I know. He helps me out when I'm short. It's hard to get dependable help these days, especially way up here." Walking to the grill, Max poured the pancake batter onto the hot surface, and put a half dozen newly cooked sausages on the back of the grill.

"More of those people still comin' into town, Allen," Max said as he worked. "Wonder where they're from and how they even find out about the place! I'd give anything to know what's behind it all."

"I don't have the slightest idea, Max. What do they do up there? Where do they all sleep? There must be at least four or five hundred of them by now."

"Tommy, the fellow from the mill, said they been ordering wood like there's no forest left."

"They seem to be nice enough folk, but not overly friendly. Keep pretty much to themselves. A little too secretive for me. They make me nervous."

"I haven't had much to do with them," Allen said. "I bump into them occasionally and say hello. They return the greeting and it ends there. I get the feeling they don't want to get chummy with anybody, as if they don't want anybody to know their business. A little scary, if you ask me. I'd love to know what they're up to."

"So would the whole town. I just hope we don't have trouble. A lot of rednecks around here who're just itchin' for a showdown with them."

Max placed the platter full of pancakes and sausages on the counter with a dish of butter. Taking the real maple syrup out of the microwave, he poured it into a small pitcher and slid it haphazardly down the counter. Joshua caught it just before it flew off the end.

"He does that every time," Allen said to Joshua, "just to make me nervous. I was waiting for it, but made believe I didn't see it. I knew you'd catch it in time."

Joshua laughed, and Max laughed, too. Allen dove into his hotcakes.

When they finished, the two left the diner and walked out into the snow. A horse and sleigh was driving past, heading for the bus station.

"There's one of those mystery people now," Allen murmured.

Joshua took off in the direction of the sleigh. Allen followed a little behind him, curious as to what he was up to.

A middle-aged man stepped down from the sleigh as Joshua approached the station.

"Hello," Joshua called out to him.

Without looking up, the man responded with a half-hearted grunt.

"That's a fine horse you have there," Joshua said, trying to draw the man into conversation.

"I don't know much about horses. Just do what I'm told."

There was something almost robotic about the man, as if he were remotely controlled and anxious about contact with strangers afraid he might be contaminated. Joshua persisted. "Where would I get a horse and sleigh like that? They are really practical up this way."

"I don't know. I just drive them."

"How can I find out? Who can I talk to?"

"Reverend Miller is director. He knows."

"Does he have a phone number?"

"We don't use phones—Satan's invention."

"How do I contact him?"

"You have to go there to visit him."

"Where is that?"

"Ten miles out the back road. Turn left at Old Mill Road. One quarter mile, that's where it is."

"Thank you."

All during the conversation, the man never once looked up at Joshua, but kept tending the horse, while waiting for the bus to come with his passengers.

The bus arrived. The man brusquely greeted the arrivals, ushered them into the sleigh, and drove off.

Joshua just stood there stunned as he watched the sleigh

leave the village and disappear into the distance. A look of concern clouded his face.

"Well, what do you think, young man?" Allen asked him.

"I'm concerned. They don't look like happy people," Joshua responded with sadness in his voice.

"They are a strange lot. Would you like to go up there?"

"Yes, I would like to meet with them," Joshua replied.

"Give me a few minutes after we get back to the house, and I'll drive you up there. It's only fifteen minutes away. Nice ride."

The road to the compound was pretty, with new snow on the trees sparkling in the sunlight like thousands of brilliant gems. Alongside the road flowed a mountain stream, partially encrusted with ice. It was a winding road, hazardous at any time of the year, but especially treacherous in winter. As they approached the compound, they were confronted by a warning posted on the side of the road: "PRIVATE, NO ENTRANCE."

Allen ignored the sign and drove through. A quarter of a mile past the entrance they came upon a construction site bustling with activity in the midst of snow. An army of workers were totally focused on putting up buildings to house the ever-increasing population of this hidden village. Judging by the varied shapes of the buildings, it appeared they were creating just that, a self-contained village, with cottages, dormitories, and stores. It was clear there were professionals among them, since the rapid pace of the work showed planning and efficient execution.

Rolling down the window, Allen called out to one of the workers, "Where can I find the Reverend Miller?"

Most of the people continued working without looking up, but one man who seemed to have some authority walked over to the car and asked what they wanted. As he did so two other men positioned themselves in front of the car.

"My friend here was told to come up and see the Reverend Miller, so I offered to drive him up. Can you tell us where we can find him?"

"His house is a little over a mile up this road. As you approach the end, turn right and go another five hundred feet. That is where the Leader lives."

The other men stepped aside, allowing the car to pass.

Allen and Joshua found the house just as the man had described—a single-story, solidly constructed bungalow. Knocking on the front door, they were greeted by the Leader himself. He appeared to be in his fifties and was of medium height, gaunt, with strong chiseled features. There was a haunted look about him, the kind of look one might associate with the prophets of old.

"Why have you come here?" he barked out, giving Allen a bit of a jolt.

"I have seen your people in the village. They seem like such nice people, and I was interested in learning more about your way of life," Joshua answered simply.

"We do have a good way of life," he said cautiously. Then after a moment sizing Joshua up, he seemed to brighten. "Would you care to come inside where we could talk?"

"Thank you," Joshua answered, following the Leader inside. In the corner a wood-burning stove glowed with heat, making the room a bit too warm.

"What a nice little house!" Allen remarked. "Did you build it yourself?"

"No. I am the Leader here. The followers designed and built it for me. They were only too happy to do it out of appreciation for all the Leader has done for them."

Joshua listened attentively and after a pause said, "You seem to be very popular."

"Yes, I have a strong message the people need to hear."

"What is that?" Joshua asked.

"We are approaching the End Times, and people should be ready. The Lord said, 'When you see the signs of the times coming, do not go up into the city, but flee into the hills.' The End Times are almost upon us, and in fact may already be upon us. The signs of the times are clear and we have taken the Lord's warning seriously. We have left the cities. We have fled into the mountains as the Lord told us to. We are building our home here knowing the Lord will protect those who heed his warning."

Joshua listened, saying nothing.

The Leader continued. "I will lead my disciples along the way of truth and righteousness. They are my children. They find peace and security in following my instructions and obeying my commands, just as the great apostle teaches, 'Obey your teachers.'"

"Well, your disciples do seem like nice people," Allen said.

"They are very good people. Once they get to know that

you have come to learn and not to find fault, they will be more open to you. You are welcome to come and visit. If you want to become a disciple, there is always room for more."

"Thank you," Joshua said, turning toward the door to leave.

"One more thing. Any attempts to undermine the faith of the followers are severely punished. I know that is not your intention, but it is just a warning. If you choose to live here, you are under my authority. We have our own government, and our own laws—laws which are religiously observed."

Allen and Joshua made their farewell and left.

Once they were back in the car the old man asked, "Well, what did you think, Joshua?"

"It is as I thought. The people have come to him because they are frightened."

"Frightened about what?"

"Frightened about many things; about the approaching millennium, and afraid that it will be the end of the world. If it is, will they be ready to meet God? The minister makes them feel secure, since he acts as if he has an in with God. That makes them feel that they are safe if they follow his directions. So, they give up everything to follow him."

"That's spooky," Allen said.

"I feel sorry for everyone here. They are just good, simple people. It is unfortunate there are those who prey on their simplicity."

As the car moved toward the exit, the same men were still there. This time they seemed a bit friendlier.

During the next few days, Joshua wandered about the

town, talking to people he met along the way, quietly becoming acquainted with the townsfolk. It was only a few days later, when he accidentally encountered the lady and the boy who were on the bus with him.

Someone had brought them down to the village to pick up provisions. When she saw Joshua, she seemed glad to have run into him.

"Hello! Aren't you the man who was on the bus the day we came up here?"

"Yes."

"I saw you the other day when you and the old man came up to visit our Leader. I would like to talk to you sometime, if it is all right."

"You can talk to me anytime."

"Well, *I* can't really talk anytime. We aren't allowed to have contact with strangers unless we are first given permission. I have only a few minutes—my ride will be coming to pick us up any time now. But I have to ask you a question. I don't know if I made the right move in coming up here, and I'm feeling more and more anxious about being here. I see you with that old man, and how kind you are to him, and I feel I can trust you. My name is Melanie. This is my son, Jonathan."

Joshua smiled down at the boy.

Walking along, Joshua listened as the woman told him some of the things that were happening at the commune. She felt there was something strange about the place, which made her feel very uncomfortable. The Leader was like a dictator. Everyone had to follow his orders exactly or they would be severely punished. The members were treated more like children than adults.

When she finished, Joshua told her that it would be better for her to go back where she came from and just continue her life as usual.

"You mean you don't think the end of the world is coming?"

"No, God does not make decisions based on people's calendar. His work of creation will not be finished for a long time. The universe is already billions of years old. That is but yesterday to my Father. He ends His work only when it is finished. As one can see, the perfecting of His creation and the maturing of His human family still have very far to go. Only people can bring about the end before it's time, but that is not in my Father's designs. So, go home and live in peace, and do not raise your child with meaningless fears. Teach him that God is a loving Father who loves him with a tender love, and that he should trust Him and not be afraid of Him. The only end you have to be concerned about is the time when God takes you home, and that will not be for a long time. So, go and enjoy your life. My Father created you to be free, and to enjoy your pilgrimage to His heavenly kingdom.

"When religion becomes a cult, people's freedom is the first thing to disappear. A cult cannot exist where people are free; free to think for themselves, free to discuss critical human issues, free to play responsible roles in the religious family to which they belong. Only cults are controlled by the few from above. In politics it is called totalitarianism. But there is no difference. Both demand total control of the human mind, and forbid freedom of discussion. Both strip people of their dignity and freedom, and not only assault the intelligence and self-respect of their members but violently tear God's family from His control, and tell the people, 'You belong to us. You will no longer form your own conscience or ask yourself what would God want. From now on we will form your conscience and tell you what we want you to think and believe, and how you are to act.' It is the desperate admission of failure by a religion that has lost the respect of its members, because it failed to lead by goodness and the intrinsic honesty of its teaching. In its place its leaders substitute intimidation and brute force in an attempt to gain the control that they could not win by honest and reasonable discussion of issues."

They had been talking just a few minutes, but it was long enough for them to be spotted by the member of the cult who had come to pick up Melanie and Jonathan. Though she felt comforted by Joshua's words, she knew the encounter would be reported. The Leader's eyes were everywhere. Melanie thanked Joshua and, taking her son's hand, walked down the street to where a sleigh was waiting for them. Joshua looked after them with sadness in his eyes. He felt the woman's desperation, trying to raise a child in a frightfully complicated world with little support from anyone. He also knew the trouble she'd created for herself by talking to him.

CHAPTER 4

WHEN MELANIE ARRIVED at the compound, it did not take long for the news to spread that she had violated the Leader's rule against speaking to strangers. Everyone shunned her and her son. But there was something else on everyone's mind—It was getting toward the end of December, the last day of the millennium was fast approaching, and there was great uncertainty. The next day could be just like any normal day, or it could be the beginning of catastrophic upheaval in the universe, with stars and sun falling from their places, and chaos causing havoc across the earth. Everyone in the compound was in a state of intense fear, and now with Melanie's transgression the future seemed all the more doubtful. Melanie could be the one to bring down the scourge of God on them all by disobeying the Leader. At all costs she needed to be isolated and repudiated as one who refused to accept good counsel and direction for her life, and the life of her son.

The Leader decided that since it was not the son's fault, he could not be blamed, but the mother was unfit to properly guide her child. His divinely inspired judgment was that the mother would be allowed to leave, but her son would stay with them, so at least he could be saved. Should she try to complain to the authorities, the Leader's followers would all agree that she had abandoned her son, and the loving family consented to care for the poor abandoned child.

Melanie was beside herself. What could she do? Who could she turn to? Suspecting she would try to kidnap the boy, the Leader had him taken to a secret cabin farther out in the woods. No one would tell her where he had been moved. If she attempted to stay among the family, she would not be accepted, which meant she would not be allowed to eat or sleep there.

That night she was forced to stay outside in the bitter cold and sleep under a tree in a makeshift shelter she had constructed out of branches and snow. The next day, hiding among the trees, she noticed two of the men walking into the woods. Quietly following them, they led her to a cabin hidden in the forest. It was obviously the place where difficult members were isolated and punished, most likely it was the place where her son was being imprisoned, to protect him from her.

Watching from a distance, she saw the men enter the cabin. The door was unlocked, which was a good sign. Whoever minded the place felt no need to lock it. Hardly five minutes passed before three men came out carrying axes and wedges. From a shed behind the cabin, one of them brought a wheelbarrow. The three then walked off into the forest.

As soon as they disappeared, Melanie ran up to the house, peeked into the windows, and saw her son sitting in a chair in the corner of the front room. He was crying. She quickly opened the door and ran to him.

"Mommy, Mommy," Jonathan called out.

"Sh-h-h, Jonathan, they might hear us. Quick, get your clothes and get dressed." Jonathan scrambled to find his winter clothes and overshoes, put them on, and quickly zippered his coat. The two of them ran out of the cabin, and down the path.

Fortunately, there were too many footprints in the packed snow for anyone to be able to follow. The two ran as fast as they could. The men would not be out cutting wood for very long. Once they returned, the whole compound would be out looking for them. They could not afford to allow them to escape.

Not only did they have to reach the highway, they had to be lucky enough to have some kind soul pick them up and drive them to the village.

As they approached the compound, Melanie had to make her first decision. Walking through the compound would be impossible. Over the past two days, she had become familiar enough with the forest to work her way around the compound and head directly for the highway. Her only fear was that when they started looking for her, it would be too easy to find their tracks in the snow. In spite of her son's weight, Marjorie picked him up and carried him, so whoever found the tracks would think it to be someone else's footprints. This she did for over almost a quarter of a mile, then, from total exhaustion, put the boy down. They both continued walking at a fast pace.

Hearing the sound of car engines, she knew she was near the highway. She also knew by intuition that the men had arrived back at the cabin, found it empty, and were already on their way to report it to the Leader.

In a state of near panic, the woman and her child reached the highway and started walking in the direction of the village. An occasional car passed, making no attempt to stop. Some had women drivers, some were men. She could understand the men being reluctant to pick her up, for a vague fear of being falsely accused of some evil intent. But she could not understand a woman, obviously seeing her panic, unwilling to help another woman so desperate, and with a little child besides. In the distance, behind her, she could hear voices coming from the direction of the compound. They were becoming more distinct as they came closer to the highway. She and her son were almost half a mile down the road.

Thank God, the highway had been recently plowed and sanded. They could not use the sleighs. But they could run faster than she and her son. Ignoring her almost total exhaustion, Melanie began running again, half dragging her crying son after her. Hearing a car approaching, she turned and quietly prayed the driver would stop. As the car approached, it slowed down and came to a halt. The driver was a boy in his late teens.

"Where you goin', ma'am?" he asked.

"Down to the village," she tried to reply while gasping for air.

"You seem to be in a bad way—what happened? Are you all right?"

"Yes, we'll be okay now, thanks to you."

"Are you coming from that crazy place up there in the woods?"

"You're right. We're trying to escape. They drove me out and tried to kidnap my son. They are really sick people up there."

"Well, you don't have to worry anymore, ma'am. We'll be in the village in a few minutes. If you plan to take a bus there will be one leaving at five-fifteen. You have two hours until then. My name is Tom, ma'am."

"Thank you, Tom. My name is Melanie. This is my son, Jonathan. What will we do when we get there? The Leader has spies all over."

"I don't know, ma'am. I can only take you as far as the village, then I have to take back roads to where I'm going. Let's see what the situation is when we reach the village. If you feel uncomfortable, maybe we can think of something else."

In the meantime, Joshua and Allen were sitting in front of the fireplace enjoying the fire. Allen was smoking his pipe. Joshua seemed distracted, as he gazed into the crackling flames. Then, rising from his chair, he excused himself.

"Allen, I'm going into town. That mother who got off the bus with me when I arrived is in trouble. She's escaped from the compound and is on her way down the highway now. There is a bus leaving at five-fifteen, which is not for two hours. We have to hide her until the bus comes. If they find her they will kidnap the two of them and drag them back up there."

"How do you know she's in trouble?"

"I have a way of understanding what's happening. I have to go out and meet them when they arrive."

"Joshua, do you really think they're that crazy up there?"

"I know they are. The Leader is a dangerous man and will stop at nothing to protect his evil schemes."

"What shall we do?"

"A young boy is driving them down the mountain road. When they enter the village, it will be dangerous because some of the Leader's people could be wandering around town."

"So, what's your plan?"

"I'll stop the car and talk to the driver. The woman and her son will recognize me, so he will be willing to listen. I will ask him to drive us back here, where they'll be safe. The young man can go on his way, while the woman and her son rest up. Later on we can drive down to the bus stop in the next town, where we can buy tickets and send the mother and her boy on their way. It would not be wise to get the tickets here, since people from the cult will probably be watching the bus station to see if she comes there."

"Joshua, I can't fathom you. How do you know they are driving down the highway?"

Joshua laughed. "I'll tell you sometime, Allen, but for now, just believe me. I'll be back in a few minutes with our guests."

"I have to admit, young man, you make my life exciting. I'll put on a pot of soup. They must both be starved."

Joshua left the house and headed for the village.

No sooner did he arrive than the car came down the road and entered the village. He walked toward it and gestured for it to stop. The driver ignored him. Then Melanie recognized Joshua.

"Oh, Tom, stop, please, he's a friend." The boy stopped and rolled down his window. Melanie seemed to forget her fears for a moment.

"Joshua! I'm so glad to see you."

"Melanie. Don't get out here. There are spies all over. Let me get in the car—I'll take you to the old man's house. He is expecting you. Then we will take you to the bus stop in the next town, where you can get your tickets and board the bus without having to worry about them finding you."

"Hop in, sir, and you can tell me where to go."

Arriving at Allen's, they all quickly went inside. Allen had the pot of soup already prepared. The smell greeted them as soon as they opened the door.

"Boy, something smells good!" Tom exclaimed.

"Just a pot of soup," Allen answered, with a proud look on his face.

"Well, sit down and tell me about this big drama we are involved in," the old man continued, with evident excitement.

When Tom heard the full picture of what happened, he felt like a real hero, and asked Joshua how he knew he was coming down the hill with the woman and her son. Joshua just laughed and made nothing of it.

Melanie wanted to give the boy some money, but he seemed offended and told her he was proud to be part of their great escape. When Allen asked if he would like to stay for a bowl of soup, he said he had to be somewhere, and was already late. But Allen wouldn't let him go that easily, and with his adamant prodding the boy finally took a quick cup of hot soup, then left.

While the others were talking, Jonathan sat quietly in front of the fireplace staring into the fire. "This is awesome!" he said. "I have never seen anything like this before, except in the movies, or on TV."

"That's the way people used to heat their homes in the old days, son," Allen told him.

"Gee, I wish we heated our house this way. It's fun."

Everyone laughed, but said nothing, allowing the boy to indulge his fantasy.

The trip to the next village bus stop was uneventful. Joshua asked Melanie what she would do when she got back home. Her apartment was still available. A relative owned the house, so she had no worry on that score. She was sure her job was still open to her, so she felt relatively secure that there would be no money problems.

"I'm glad that I didn't turn my money over to that phony. I thought there was something bizarre going on from the moment I arrived at the place, so I waited before I gave them any money. Now I'll be in good shape when I get back home. Jonathan is still on vacation, so he hasn't missed any school."

The bus arrived on schedule. There was a great sense of relief for Allen and Joshua when the door closed and the bus started down the highway. They had barely seen a soul since they left Allen's house; no one followed them on the highway; no one suspicious-looking had been at the store where the bus made its stop. Except for an elderly lady, there was no one else waiting for the bus. Their relief complete, Allen and Joshua drove back to the house.

"You know, Joshua, you seem like a quiet, detached, peaceful man. But I can't understand how such a calm personality as yours can so easily get caught up in these action dramas. Even the day you came into town, you saved me from being run over by a truck. And now this woman and her child. Is your whole life like this?"

"Allen, you are in many ways like a little child. You have that childlike simplicity Jesus talked about. That is why I made your acquaintance when I came to town. I know you don't go to church very often, but your heart is pure and your life is honest, and you talk to God in the only way you know, from your heart. When you do go to church, you sit in the back, like the repentant man in the back of the temple, asking God to pardon your failings and your sins. Your humility has touched my Father's heart. You are a kind, compassionate man. You are poor because you chose to give so much of what you had during your life to those who had nothing. I knew I could trust myself to you."

"Young man, how do you know all these things about me? You just met me!"

"Allen, I knew you before you were born."

"I believe it. But how? Who? Oh, my God, no!"

"Yes, Allen, but do not be frightened. Just be the good person you are and relax. I have come to visit because I have no place to stay in this cold weather, and I need your friendship."

"You need my friendship. How could you need my friendship? I have nothing I could give you. Everything I have is yours. I don't understand."

"All those people up in the mountain. They are like simple sheep being led to the slaughter. They are in danger of being destroyed. They need our help. I need you to work with me to help them."

"Well, Joshua, I wish I knew how I should treat you, but I'm sorry, I only know how to be myself."

"That's why I came to visit you, because I knew you would be yourself. So, be at peace."

"You know, Joshua, I have to admit, you do make life fun."

"My Father is a fun God. He created people so they could enjoy the life He dreamed of for them. You call it fun. Yes, you could say my Father wanted people to have fun."

Allen, knowing now who Joshua was, felt honored that he should need *him,* of all people, to help in this important work. He was looking forward to the possibilities of what might happen. If the intrigue of spiriting the woman and her child out of the village was any example, it was going to be very exciting. The old man had found a new reason to live besides meeting his friends for breakfast at the diner. What he could not figure out, however, was how Joshua intended to dismantle the cult community up in the mountain. He went to bed that night dreaming about the place, and his role in it.

THE NEXT DAY, New Year's, the whole cult community was astir with murmuring about what had happened, and how the woman and her child escaped. The fact that she had so easily left showed a flaw in the community's "educational" process. Granted the woman had been there only a couple of days, but she had been "educated" for weeks by the local devotees in the place where she and her child lived. They thought she had been readied and properly programmed. But they were mistaken. Guilt at betraying the Leader and the cult family should have kicked in at the first thought of abandoning the family. Guilt is the glue that holds cults together, and cements unquestioning loyalty to the Leader. This psychological hold on members' minds could often be total. There is no room for personal decisions, or independent thinking. The guilt that arises when one even begins to question either a teaching or an order or an issue freezes any further deliberation. That is why it is so difficult to help people who are victims of cults. Talking to such a programmed person is like talking to a mindless automaton. This happens often in religion, even in isolated groups of mainstream religious groups, where a leader so dominates the thinking of the members that they no longer think for themselves. "This is what my pastor told me. This is what I have been taught, and I cannot question it." That kind of thinking and training is the beginning of cultic behavior.

The Leader was angry that morning, because the woman's escape had distracted the community from what it was supposed to be focused on, the beginning of the year, and the frightening, and possibly catastrophic imminence of the new millennium. How could they allow themselves to be so easily distracted?

Late in the morning the Leader called an assembly of the whole community. They met in the new meeting hall. There were no chairs or, indeed, any furniture of any kind. The people sat on the floor. The Leader stood up front on a slightly raised platform.

When he began to speak, a breathless silence descended on the room. "My children," he began, "this is a soul-wrenching day, a day when all the past will be destroyed and a new world will emerge for each of you. It is a day when you should consider the last day of your life, for indeed, this could be the last day of your life. How shocked I was, my children, that, after all my teaching and preparation for this day, you could still allow yourselves to be distracted by the ingratitude and treachery of that woman, who is bringing not only herself but her offspring to destruction. We tried to save at least the child, but because of the negligence of some of you, she was able to steal the child from us, and escape. And that man, that man who was caught talking to her. He is the evil one. Beware of him! He seduced her mind and tore her from our midst. Avoid him as you would avoid Satan himself. When you see him in the village, do not even look at him. His very eyes will bewitch you. But enough of that man and that woman!

"We must think of our purpose and our mission. Remember that we are the remnant, the few who will survive the devastation and misery that is about to befall our planet. When you see the stars of the heavens quivering, and the earth quaking, and strange things happening in nature, the time, that terrible time, is upon us. You, however, who have chosen to follow me, will be saved all this anxiety and destruction. You are the chosen ones. Because you have chosen to give up all to follow me you will be spared. Under my protection you are safe.

"Before this meeting breaks up, I must warn you. Do not even think of the terrible thing that woman did in leaving us. Do not entertain thoughts of disloyalty and ingratitude. I have given up my life to save you and to be your Leader. Be loyal and dedicated to me, as I am loyal and totally dedicated to you. Now go and continue with your appointed tasks."

Though many in the family were educated, some having laid aside important positions to follow their Leader, they obeyed without questioning, like children learning for the first time how to live. What is it that bewitches seemingly intelligent people to surrender their freedom and even their consciences to obey the wishes of such a person? Is it their need for the mother or father they never had, one who will offer them a chance to relive their childhood and feel the security and comfort of being loved, as long as they obey? Whatever the reason, these people now act like little children, not the kind of children Jesus talked about in the gospels, but the kind of make-believe children who are willing to abandon personal responsibility to follow a clever religious fraud leading them to destruction. Jesus had warned of people like that who would come in sheep's clothing prophesying imminent doom, and would try to lead the sheep astray. He warned his disciples not to follow them.

Joshua had felt the evil presence as soon as he entered the village. And the Leader felt his presence as well, and was preparing his disciples to resist him.

While the Reverend and his followers were busy working, Joshua and Allen had slept late that morning. For Joshua it was just another day. The calendar had no meaning to him.

At breakfast, however, Joshua took a piece of bread and poured a small glass of wine. Allen watched and wondered, "What is this man up to now?"

Then Joshua took the bread, broke it into two pieces, and raised his eyes and offered a prayer. "Father, bless this village and everyone in it. Bless my kind friend, who welcomed me into his home. We thank you that he has lived and survived another year. Bless him with good health until his work here on earth is finished."

Then, looking at Allen, he said to him, "Take this. This is

my body that has been offered up for you and for the world." He then gave him the cup and said to him, "Take this cup. It is the cup of my blood, which has been shed for you and for others for their eternal salvation."

The old man recognized what Joshua was doing from his stops by the local church to pray while the Eucharist was being offered. But he felt that this was even more real than what happened in church. He felt so honored. Tears came to the old man's eyes and ran down his cheeks. He cried unashamedly as he took the Bread and the Wine and consumed it. His look into Joshua's eyes said more than a thousand expressions of gratitude. Joshua did not consume what he had just blessed, for he was what he had just consecrated.

The two men laughed and cajoled each other during breakfast over the events of the past few days. Allen was bursting with curiosity over the strategy he knew was taking shape behind that calm, impenetrable facade with the playful grin. Joshua knew Allen was dying to ask him what was going to happen next. All Joshua would tell him was that he should not be nervous or anxious, as no harm would come. This piqued the old man's curiosity even more.

As in the old days, Jesus was without fear. He brought the battle into the midst of the enemy camp. It was just before noon when Joshua had Allen drive him to the commune. As the community was not expecting visitors, there was no one near the entrance. They drove right through and parked the car not far from the dining hall.

"Stay here, Allen, while I do what I must do," Joshua told him, knowing full well that the old man could not resist seeing what he was about to do.

Joshua walked straight up to the dining hall. As soon as he entered, there was a stunned silence. Even the Leader was shocked, whether because of the boldness of the man, or by the majestic presence of the enemy, he sat in his place at the table with his mouth open and his eyes glued to this overwhelming presence that had in a single moment mesmerized his whole community of followers.

Then, coming to his senses, he screamed out in such a strange guttural voice that even his followers were shocked. "What do you want with us? We know who you are. You have come to destroy us."

Joshua looked across the heads of the people toward the table where the Leader was sitting. The man's face had a wild look about it. The evil that he managed to keep hidden now broke through the mask and frightened everyone near him.

"Be silent," Joshua commanded him. "I know you from the days of old, father of lies. You have bewitched and deceived these good and honest people looking for a way to find God. Your tricks may have changed, but your cunning lays its traps to ensnare the innocent. In the past you were obvious, evil one. Now you try to mimic God, feigning to gather God's children together, so you might lead them to God. But, in reality, you are leading them to the very brink of hell.

"I know you from before the days when you fell like lightning from heaven. You have not changed, Lucifer. The brilliance of your mind still dazzles the unwary and the simple, but behind your every step, my messengers are there to counter each of your moves."

The Leader sat there speechless, looking ridiculous, as saliva drooled down from the corner of his open mouth. It was as if his face was frozen in a spasm of hatred.

Joshua turned toward the crowd, who still did not know what to do. "You have come here to find peace and security. But you will find only evil and pain. You are good people and were already close to God. You do not have to worry about today or the days to come. God does not made decisions according to your human calendars. Today and this year is just another day and another year. Remember, you are the children of God, beloved and cared for by a Father in heaven who loves you with a tenderness you could never even begin to understand. Do not allow yourselves to be trapped again into bondage. You have been freed by the blood of your Savior, who redeemed you from slavery and brought you into a new life of freedom. Do not surrender that freedom to false prophets who do the devil's work, trying to seduce you back into bondage once again.

"Look at what has happened to you since you came here. You are no longer free to think for yourselves. You are not even free to follow your conscience. When you try to, you are punished and made to feel ashamed. That is not what your Father in heaven wants for you. That is not what your Savior died for. You were redeemed so you could be free and enjoy the life the Father has destined for you. Walk away from this place and go back to your families and your homes, and begin your lives all over again."

While all this was going on, Allen left the car and walked over to a window where he could see and hear everything.

When Joshua finished, the Reverend tried to speak, but

the din was overwhelming. The crowd broke into loud discussion among themselves. Three women and a man sitting close to Joshua went over to him and asked him who he was.

"No one has ever talked like you. You sound like something out of the gospel itself. Who are you?"

"I have given my life for you, and have purchased you at a great price. I will not allow the evil one to tear you away a second time from my Father. Leave here and go in peace."

They were deeply touched and told their friends that they thought he must be a messenger from God. "Look at his face!" said a young lady in her late twenties. "It looks so noble. His eyes are kind and full of compassion. He seems sincere. I think he may be right. I've never felt peace in this place ever since I came here. I'm getting out of here."

Those with her agreed and rose to leave the dining hall. Some of the Leader's staunchest followers were furious and tried to stop the group from leaving. As they approached the group, however, Joshua turned and stood between them. The henchmen stopped abruptly. The threatening look on Joshua's face dazed them. He had no weapon, no one to protect him, but his look alone held them at bay.

The small group walked past untouched, and left the building. Many others followed. "Hurry, get your belongings and leave here," Joshua told them. "Take what money is rightfully yours and leave this place immediately."

As long as Joshua stayed there, an uncanny power seemed to chain the evil that enveloped the place. The almost three hundred who decided to stay were powerless to prevent the others from leaving.

Joshua waited for several minutes as the ones who were

leaving picked up their few belongings. When he saw them walking down the road toward the entrance, he turned and left the building. Allen was standing near the car when Joshua approached. With a broad grin, he opened the door for Joshua, who just looked at him and smiled back.

As they drove past the people who were leaving, Allen asked Joshua what had taken place.

"Oh, nothing terribly exciting," Joshua replied. "I said a few words to the crowd. Some liked what I said and decided to leave. The rest stayed."

"Well, weren't the others angry?" Allen asked, trying hard to pretend not to know.

"I suppose they were. But they did nothing about it," Joshua said casually, waiting for Allen to make a slip and betray himself.

"Well, why were they so quiet? I didn't hear a sound."

"They probably did not know what happened. It was all so sudden."

"No, I mean when the group got up to leave. The others couldn't stop them. What happened?"

"Oh, is that what happened? I hadn't noticed," Joshua answered with a broad grin, knowing he had checkmated his friend.

Allen finally confessed. "Well, Joshua, I couldn't resist. I was peeking through the window and saw the whole thing. You were absolutely marvelous. Is that what you were like in the old days, as you say? Did you stand up in front of crowds like that in front of your enemies, just as cool and unafraid? No wonder the people followed you everywhere. You must have been like a living television drama, with each day a new episode. No one knew what to expect next. Just watching you makes the gospels all of a sudden seem like an adventure."

Joshua looked at Allen and smiled. "Allen, you know, you truly are like a little child."

"Well, remember, that's why you chose me to work with you."

"I know."

"Where do we go now?"

"Down to the bus stop, to tell the agent to call for two more buses to cope with the emergency. Then, let's just take a nice ride in the country to relax and stop at a little restaurant for an early supper. Aren't you tired? I know I am."

"Aha, you can still get tired? That's interesting. I thought that once you, you, well, you know what I mean, that once you went over there, you know, to the other side, you no longer got tired."

"Face it, Allen, the body requires energy, whether it's the body you have or the one I now have. It is the form of energy that baffles you. I require energy, though I do not process it the way you do. Remember the roasted fish the night of the Resurrection? I ate that and it was all consumed and converted into energy."

"Oh well, that makes sense, I guess. I just thought, well, I guess I just never thought much about it. But I'm learning." And he began to figure that, in some way, food Joshua consumed was converted into whatever type of energy animated him.

The countryside on the cold sunny afternoon was restful and charming. The old homesteads were set back from the highway, with lights flickering in the windows and smoke floating up from the chimneys, creating a warm, nostalgic mood. It was a peaceful ride. The old man had never known such joy and contentment. To sit next to such a Person who considered you a friend and partner would be any human's dream.

Darkness settled late in the afternoon as the mountainpeaks and tall trees hid the cold winter sun. It was not late when they reached the village. On the way three buses passed them on the highway.

"They must be the people from the commune," Allen said with triumphant glee in his voice.

"Yes, they are now free. Just pray they do not fall back into the fear that drew them here in the first place. People do not know how much my Father loves them. They have such a need to be affirmed and loved. Unfortunately, they embrace it wherever they find it, even if it leads them back into darkness."

Once back at the house, Joshua suggested they start a fire in the fireplace. "I like to sit and watch the fire. It is so relaxing and soothing."

"Joshua, you amaze me. You enjoy being human, don't you?"

"Yes, it's fun. My Father made things that way, so His children could find pleasure in His creation and see His love reflected in everything He made. It makes my Father sad when He sees how people carelessly destroy the land, and all the beautiful things He created. Thoughtless people will eventually bring an end to life on earth if they do not show respect for the delicate balance my Father has built into His creation. Everything in creation is built on complex relationships that are necessary to preserve balance and stimulate the unending development of life."

"I think you lost me on that one, young man. Remember, I never really went too far in school. But I'm trying to understand what you mean. If we don't take care of the environment, we're goin' to pay a heavy price one day."

"You put it nicely, Allen. See, you've learned a lot in your lifetime. You went to a real good school, and learned well."

Allen made a pot of coffee, and the two sat before the fireplace, sometimes chatting, sometimes just staring into the mesmerizing flames of the fire, until they both fell off to sleep.

CHAPTER 6

AS THE DAYS passed, people's curiosity about Joshua increased. Word about the exodus from the commune spread through the village and, indeed, throughout the whole hill country. Whenever he went into town, people would stop him and question him about what he thought of the goings-on there. Joshua was always polite, but spoke in generalities usually, as was his custom. "People need understanding. The reason why they are attracted to groups like that is because they find acceptance, an acceptance one rarely finds in churches. People need one another for strength and reassurance. That was what Jesus intended when he brought the Good News, but often his followers are not accepting of people who are troubled and hurting. While we worry about groups like this, what are we willing to offer people who need our help and understanding?" That was pretty much what Joshua had to say when he was questioned, leaving his questioners perplexed and feeling not a little ashamed or embarrassed because they, for the most part, had bad feelings about those strange people invading what they considered their private preserve, their own mountain retreat.

Again, as so often before, clergy began to show concern. Who is this stranger who just walks into town and involves himself in the religious affairs of the community? These are the Church's concern, what business is it of his?

Two of the clergy actually approached him one day and asked him precisely those questions; by what authority did he do the things he was doing? It probably would have been more gracious if they had invited him to one of their homes for dinner and, with a few priests and ministers, discussed the commune with him in a respectful and concerned way. But, as in the past, it was easier, for some reason, to confront him in the street, while he was talking to others. And that is just what happened.

A portly, middle-aged minister and a gray-haired priest in his early sixties approached the little group surrounding Joshua. They were enjoying lighthearted conversation, and were individuals who had apparently developed a warm relationship with him over the past few days.

"What a surprise bumping into you on our way to the store!" the minister interjected.

Joshua turned and looked at him, but said nothing. He knew it was not a chance encounter, and waited for what was coming next. The group was taken aback at the interruption, but they also said nothing, which made the clergy-men feel rather awkward.

"We were just on our way to the store and were surprised to see you all standing here having a good time. Thought we would join the friendly conversation," the priest said.

A man in the group who had been talking with Joshua, broke in and introduced the clergymen to Joshua. "Joshua, these are two of our outstanding clergy in town. Paul Cashin, our local Methodist pastor, and John Keeler, the resident Catholic priest. Gentlemen, this is Joshua, whom, I take it, you already know, if not personally, at least by hear-say."

The three men extended their hands in greeting. "Welcome to town," the two clergymen said almost in unison.

"Thank you. It is a beautiful town. The people have been so gracious," Joshua replied.

"Word around town is that you created quite a stir up in the commune a few days ago. How did you manage to get involved with them?" Father Keeler asked Joshua.

"Just ordinary concern of one human being for another," Joshua retorted pleasantly.

"Why would you be concerned?" the priest continued.

"Because I could see and understand things that I knew were not healthy about the group, and could be quite harmful to the people."

"Don't you think that would have been better left to the clergy in the area, since it deals with religious matters?" Reverend Cashin asked.

"Religion is everyone's concern; where clergy lack leadership people are left to assuming the initiative. If I thought the clergy intended to do something, I would not have become involved. If you had been taking steps to protect the people, then I was mistaken. Might I ask you what measures you have taken so far? My friends here are quite involved in your churches, and they might be interested in knowing."

Embarrassed, the two clergymen fumbled for an answer, but realizing the audience knew that they had never even discussed the matter, they were at a loss for words, and quickly changed the subject to what a beautiful day it was turning out to be.

When they left, Joshua's little group went back to their original discussion, which was where Joshua had been before he came to their village, and what kind of work he had been involved in. Of course, Allen was laughing to himself, wondering how Joshua was going to get out of that one.

Never lost for an answer, Joshua simply replied, "My family is independent, and I spend much of my time traveling."

Allen shook his head and smiled at Joshua's clever response.

A few minutes later the group broke up. Joshua and Allen continued on their walk.

"Joshua, you never cease to amaze me. You really put those two fellows in their place. And you did it with such grace.

"Joshua, how will you handle the rest of the people at the commune? Will you go up there again?"

"No, I think not. People will drift down to the village to talk to us, and in time we will show some of them their way to freedom. But not all. There are some who are still bound up with fear and feel more secure in their bondage than in being free. They are afraid of freedom. Those I cannot help, because they are not open. The ones who come to visit I will help, then I will move on."

In fact, later that afternoon, a few people from the commune did come to visit; a young family of five, a father and mother and three children. The parents were in their late thirties, the children ranged from twelve to six. Allen and Joshua were sitting in front of the fireplace, chatting and drinking hot chocolate, when there was a knock at the door. Allen got up to answer it and was surprised to see the little family standing there, looking so hopeless, and helpless too, one might add.

"May we come in, sir? We would like to talk to Joshua, if he is at home," the father said, with touching humility.

"Come right in, come right in. In fact, I think Joshua was expecting you."

"Really," the man replied. "He must have read our minds."

"He's good at that," Allen said with a broad grin revealing empty spaces where there were once back teeth. The old man was finally beginning to feel comfortable enough with Joshua to take playful liberties in his comments, showing the pride he felt in their friendship.

Joshua stood up and walked to greet the guests as they entered the living room.

"My name is Harold," the man said as he introduced

himself. "This is my wife Geraldine. These are our children, Jacob, Emily, and Sarah."

The children, without prompting, held out their hands to shake Joshua's. One could see they were a well-bred and very proper family.

"I am pleased you came to visit," Joshua said. "Allen is our gracious host who just welcomed you."

"Hello, Allen. It is a pleasure to meet you. We are grateful to you for allowing us to come and talk with Joshua. He has had a great impact on our lives since the day he spoke to us at the commune. It took a lot for us to make the decision to come down here today. I hope we did the right thing."

"Come and sit down," Allen said. There were enough chairs for the adults. Allen directed the children to a long bench along the wall left of the fireplace. The fire was roaring as it shot up the chimney. The children were immediately mesmerized.

"I don't know where to start," Harold began. "My wife and I had been concerned about the way the world is moving, and we have been worried about our children, and where they should group up. No place seems right for them. No matter where one lives there are dangers and such horrible things taking place. Where does one raise children today?

"We heard the Reverend Miller speak on the radio last year. He spoke about this village he was building. It would be for people who wanted to raise their children in a safe environment, where they would be protected from the terrible things that were going to take place in the year two thousand. When we heard him we felt, both my wife and I, that we should sign up and become part of what seemed to be a dream place for Christian families. It seemed the answer to our prayer.

"But, then, after being with this group for the past three months, we found that it is not quite like the dream place he described. It is frightening. When you spoke to us that day, Joshua, you opened our eyes. We had been wondering, but were afraid to question, almost felt guilty for not trusting this man who seemed only to want the best for people. You made us see what was really happening. We were being led back into bondage, where we were no longer able to be ourselves and to express our own thoughts and feelings. We had to mouth what the Reverend wanted us to say, and never disapprove or disagree. That would be ungrateful and disloyal.

"Each day we learned of new things he wanted us to accept. Even the kinds of clothes he told us to wear. We had to take baths only at certain times. We could not buy anything without his permission. He wanted us to turn over all our money to his assistants, and they would give us money as they judged we needed it. Fortunately, I held back and turned in only a fraction of what I had with me. In his clever strategy, the Reverend was slowly and subtly alienating the children from their parents, teaching them to be loyal to him, and to report to him any disloyalty on the part of their parents. That was when I finally realized that there was something not healthy about this whole thing.

"Geraldine, however, feels guilty about my thinking this way, even though she has experienced the same thing. What we are now doing she considers disloyalty to the man, whom she thinks means well, but is misguided. Joshua, can you help us? We are so confused."

"I understand your pain and your confusion. When a person lives in fear and is overwhelmed with anxiety, it is difficult to see the path before you. I know you want what is best for your children and are willing to make great sacrifices for them. But you cannot run away from the world without creating a nightmare for yourselves. There is nothing evil about the world my Father has created. If you teach your children values that are true, and guide them by your own example, they will withstand the onslaught of evil around them. And remember, your heavenly Father sends his angels to watch over the little ones so evil will not touch them. Go back home and continue the lives you have left behind. You have good families and friends to support you, and do not worry needlessly about the children. They are God's children. He has merely loaned them to you. He is more concerned about them than you ever could be, so leave them in His hands, and trust His goodness and His love. Go in peace."

It was only a few words Joshua spoke to them. Was it the authority in his voice, or were their hearts already open to him, so that those few words were all they needed to convince them of what they should do? They thanked Joshua profusely for sharing with them his wisdom and for setting their hearts at rest.

"Now we can leave in peace." Geraldine had tears in her eyes, as she walked over to her husband and held tightly to his arm. She needed to hear what Joshua had said to them.

They thanked Allen for his hospitality and walked toward the door.

"Can I drive you somewhere?" Allen asked them.

"No, we are not going back to that place. What we left up there can be replaced. We have all we need in each other. The bus will be here in a half hour. That will give us plenty of time to get our tickets and make sure we get seats. Thank you both for all your help."

Joshua stood in the doorway and watched them as they walked down the path to the sidewalk, and waved a last good-bye. There was a sadness in his eyes as he thought of all the fear and confusion that burdened people's lives. "If only people could trust, and know that my Father loves them and wants only a chance to show His care for them. But they are too afraid to let Him into their lives, so they are trapped by the evil they see all around them, with no escape."

"Joshua, you really puzzle me," Allen said as he watched him.

"Why, friend?"

"Because you are such a happy person, and you have the whole universe under your control, but there is still a sadness about you that I find hard to understand. You really worry about people, don't you. I never thought of God as worrying about anything."

"Allen, it is not really worry, but a feeling of sadness, because we love so much. I wept over my people in Jerusalem, because I saw the tragedy about to befall them. My Father and I care very much. We do not worry, because worry is about fear of the unknown, and everything is known to us. Sadness is the pain one feels for a loved one who suffers some tragedy. That sadness is very real to me, and to my Father as well."

"How can God be sad? I can't understand that."

"Because our love is deep. When we gave free will to people, my Father tied his hands behind his back, so to speak. As a result, we endure the evil that people bring upon themselves and others. We know that when they arrive home, their joy in heaven will be in proportion to the pain and misery they endured here, but our love still compels us to grieve over their pain and tragedy. Remember, Allen, just because God is omnipotent, it does not mean that He is inert, and without feeling. God is limitless energy and passion. His love is passion, and like all love, it suffers pain."

"If God can feel everyone's pain, how can he endure it?"

"That you will not be able to understand, my friend. God does not become emotionally involved in grief. He feels people's pain, but his vision into the future sees the ultimately happy resolution of people's suffering, so the pain passes and cannot be measured in the way humans measure pain."

"You're right, I cannot understand that. That's way beyond me, but I believe you."

In the next few days more people from the commune came to visit Joshua, and through his guidance found their way back to reality. But the Leader was becoming more and more incensed over Joshua's undermining his grand scheme. He had his most loyal followers convinced that Joshua was the anti-Christ, and must be destroyed before he undid all the Leader's wonderful work to save people from destruction.

So, one day, while Joshua was at breakfast with Allen in the village café, a man passed by his place at the counter. While Joshua was engrossed in conversation, he slipped something into Joshua's cup, and kept walking. When Joshua finished talking, he called the waiter and asked him to pour out the drink and give him another cup.

"Is there something wrong with it, Joshua?"

"When you gave it to me, no, but a man passing by put something into it while I was talking."

"Did you see who it was?"

"I know who it is, but it need not concern anyone. I will take care of that."

"Did you see the guy, Allen?" the waiter asked.

"I saw a fellow pass by, but I didn't pay much attention to him. I have seen him in the past with people from the commune."

The waiter brought Joshua another cup of chocolate. "Enjoy, Joshua. I didn't put as much coffee in it this time. It should taste better."

"It really wasn't the drink, Johnny. There is something bad in it."

Two days later, the same man, but this time with a companion, accosted Joshua as he was walking up the isolated path to Allen's house. They leapt out of the shrubs, and as they were about to stab him, their hands became paralyzed, and the knives dropped to the ground. When they realized what had happened to them, they panicked and fled, their paralyzed arms dangling as they ran. Their disability would only be temporary, but their fright would last a long time.

Two days later when Allen and Joshua went to the café for breakfast, the waiter came over to them and quietly told Joshua, "You know that cup of chocolate coffee you said was bad, well, I had a friend bring it to work the next day. Guess what he found!"

Joshua just listened.

"Strychnine, deadly. Joshua, how did you know?"

"Maybe a sixth sense," he replied.

In the few days that followed a good number of people came from the commune to visit Joshua. On one occasion eighteen people showed up, some seriously damaged over what they had gone through; all deeply troubled by their experiences. Joshua comforted them and gave them the encouragement they needed to make the final break with the cult.

His work finally finished, he made his preparation to depart. Not all the members of the commune saw the light. The hard core remained steadfast in their loyalty to the Leader. Joshua knew he could do no more.

Allen, while feeling lost at the thought of losing his dear friend, knew he could not cling to him, and as sad as the departure was, bade Joshua farewell as he dropped him off at the bus terminal in the next town. Joshua thanked the old man profusely for his friendship and his important help in saving so many people's lives.

CHAPTER 7

JOSHUA MISSED THE old man as he sat back and reminisced over all that had happened in the last few weeks. The fellow had been humble and discreet enough to respect Joshua's privacy and keep the secret of his identity to himself. Now he could not tell anyone, for who would believe him? They would think he was going "soft in the head," as the Irish say. He had no need to share it with anyone anyway. The secret treasured in his heart was all the comfort and assurance he needed that he and God were friends.

As Joshua was traveling a long distance this time, it was necessary to change buses on several occasions. Through each place he passed, he sensed the fear that hung like a leaden cloud over the area, so strong was the presence of evil trying to gain a foothold through people's insecurity and lead them astray. Joshua prayed for each community as the bus drove by.

It took two days for the bus to arrive at his destination. It was a Midwestern town, and oddly enough the residence of one of the people whom Joshua rescued from the commune. It seemed as if Joshua had staged this trip, like the trip he planned long ago to meet the Samaritan woman at the well. Riding the bus that distance, which was so unlike his style, gave him a chance to pass through many cities and villages along the way, sense their fears and hopes and pray for each as he passed. Exiting the bus, he walked to the TV station, where he knew his contact worked.

When he asked to see the person (her name was Sally Blair), he was told to be seated and she would be with him in a few minutes. She was presently on the air. What a surprise when she came out and saw Joshua sitting in the waiting room!

"Joshua, what are you doing way out here? How good to see you! I owe my life to you. I hope you know that. By the way, have you ever been on TV?"

"No."

"Would you like to be?"

"I think it could be very worthwhile."

"You don't look like the kind who would get nervous."

"No, I enjoy speaking to people, as you know."

"Let me introduce you to my boss. I have already told him about you. Come with me."

Sally led Joshua down the hall to the director's office.

"Sally, come right in. Who's your friend?"

"This is the man I told you about when I came back from my little episode with that commune. His name is Joshua."

"Oh yes. Well, you certainly did us all a great favor by getting our Sally back to us. She's very valuable and extremely popular throughout our whole channel area. My name is Charlie Black, by the way."

The two men shook hands

Then, gesturing to Joshua and Sally, "Won't you sit down?

"Sally told me about your courageous act in entering the commune dining room and exposing the sham of the cult Leader in front of his own people. That must have taken a lot of courage. Why did you feel so impelled to do such a thing?"

"It should not be looked upon as extraordinary for people to help others in trouble. We live in a time when people are more confused than ever, and fall easy prey to charlatans. It was nothing extraordinary what I did."

"Maybe for you, Joshua, the extraordinary is normal. For most people what you did would be nothing short of heroic."

"Now, Sally, I know you didn't bring Joshua in here just so we could say hello. What did you have in mind?"

"Well, Charles, you know, with all the concern about the millennium, and how people are so caught up in it, many on the verge of panic, I thought Joshua would be perfect for an interview. His ideas on the millennium and on what's happening all over are so healthy. As you can see, he's a natural."

"How do you feel about being on TV, Joshua?"

"I have no problem with that at all. It would be a good chance to speak to people about so many things that trouble them, especially now when so many are worrying about the end of the world being imminent."

"When would you like to do it, Sally?"

"I would like to have a day or two to plan it and promote it, so as many people as possible could view it, and call in with their questions and concerns."

"How much time will you need?"

"At least an hour."

"An hour? In two days, impossible."

"But, Charlie, once people see him on the air, they will tell all their friends, and I know from hearing Joshua speak, he will have the audience spellbound. If you're worried about the advertising, maybe we could call our clients and ask if they would like to advertise on Joshua's time. They will sure get their money's worth."

"Are you absolutely certain it will be as riveting as you think it will be?"

"Absolutely certain."

"Okay, Sally. You've never been wrong yet. But make sure it's well promoted on the news for the next two days, morning, noon, and night, and late night. It was a pleasure meeting you, Joshua. Good luck with your introduction to TV."

Sally and Joshua went to Sally's office where they discussed details of what they might talk about on the program. Joshua was excited about the prospect of speaking to so many people over a medium such as television. He had been interviewed years before, but this was a major program and would profoundly affect the lives of everyone who would be watching it.

"Now, Joshua, let's get down to details. Where will you be staying?"

"I haven't made any plans."

"You mean you have no friends here and no place to stay? Well, why did you come all the way out here? Not just to see me?"

"Yes. That was the only reason."

"I don't believe it. And you knew I would ask you to do an interview, I suppose?"

"Yes."

"But how did you know I worked on television?"

"In the same way I understand many things. Some might call it intuition."

"And you even knew the city where I live without my ever telling you. Well, Joshua, I'm not going to pursue that any farther. But you certainly impress me. Yes, this is going to be one blockbuster of an interview. I can't wait for it myself now. Wait till you see the questions I'll have for you. We're going to have some real fun, if, of course, you don't mind."

"Not at all. I am also looking forward to it. In fact, I am excited about it."

"We'll have to make arrangements for you to stay at a local motel, a nice one, of course. Would you mind that? Unless you wouldn't mind staying with our family? I'm sure my husband would be delighted to see you again. He'll have a thousand questions to ask you, and he's not working the rest of the week, so he could entertain you."

"I'd like that rather than the motel."

"Good, so it's all set then. If you don't mind waiting, I'll be finished in about a half hour. Just relax here in my office while I take care of a little business."

The drive to Sally's house was a pleasure. She lived in the country with her husband and two daughters. The countryside was flat and the fields on either side of the highway stretched way back to the horizon. This was mid-America and there were no mountains, only vast stretches of farmland, or what used to be farmland, before the city sprawl swallowed up all the vacant land. But the scenery was, in its own way, exciting, with large farmhouses set back from the road in groves of trees, often with a stream running past the house.

"Have you ever played golf, Joshua?"

"Hardly."

"I think you'd be good at it."

"I think it could be fun, if it's not taken too seriously. I have heard a lot of jokes about God, and Moses, and Jesus playing golf. Moses would be good at it, very determined, real competitive. There are certainly enough places to play around here. We passed three courses already."

Sally's house was set back from the highway, with a long, winding driveway lined with Lombardy poplars. The house was an old brick colonial. Columns in front framed the car port, sheltering the entrance from the rain and snow. As

Sally's car approached the house, two young girls ran across the lawn to the car port and waited.

When Sally got out of the car, the girls ran over to her and hugged her. "Mommy, we're so glad you're home. We have so many things to tell you."

"Girls, you remember Joshua."

The girls looked at him, not knowing how to react. They had seen him at the commune when he spoke, but the time there was so stressful and oppressive, they had blotted everything about it from their memory. Joshua's presence brought it all back and the children's mixed feelings showed in the strange way they looked at Joshua.

"Hello, Joshua. We remember you. You spoke to all those people," the younger girl said.

"Yes, I am very happy to see you again, and you all look so happy. You missed your mother, didn't you?"

"Yes, we always miss her. She's our best friend. We love it when she comes home at night. We watch her on television, but that's not the same."

"Joshua, I had better tell you their names before they get talking. They'll never stop. This is Sarah, my baby. And this is Carlie. Sarah is my clinger. Carlie is her daddy's girl, for this week anyway. Every now and then they switch, and keep us both guessing which one is my pet today."

"They sure are loved. It is easy to tell that."

"Mommy, we have a surprise for you," Sarah blurted out.

"Oh, what's that?"

"It's a surprise. We can't tell you."

"You can't even give me a hint?"

"Not even a hint," Carlie said.

"Mommy, bend down so I can whisper something to you," Sarah said.

"What is it, Sarah?" Sally asked as she bent down.

"It's cookies, Mommy. We baked them all by ourselves."

"Darn it, Sarah, you agreed not to tell."

"I'm sorry, I just couldn't wait. It's still a surprise, whether we told her now, or whether she found out inside. This is sort of like a preview. But she'll still be happy when she sees them, because they're wonderful."

Inside the house, Sally's husband, Frank, greeted them. "Welcome home, dear. You got a lot of phone calls today. None seem so important they can't wait. Joshua, what are you doing way out in this godforsaken country? Welcome, anyway, no matter what storm brought you in. I never dreamed I would see you again after that frightening experience in the mountains. You are most welcome here."

Ordinarily, children were immediately drawn to Joshua, but these children's memories of Joshua were associated with unpleasant happenings in their lives that they could not relate to him right away. Besides, they were so absorbed in their cookies, nothing else was important.

"Um-m-m, these are good," Sally said as she tasted her daughters' chocolate chip cookies. "Would you like one, Joshua? I have to admit, I can't imagine you eating chocolate chip cookies."

"You would be surprised at what I eat," he replied.

"Sally, I also decided to surprise you," Frank interjected.

"You won't have to worry about supper tonight. I have reservations for dinner at six-thirty, in honor of our anniversary."

"Anniversary?" Sally replied, totally caught off guard.

"Yes, our anniversary. I can't believe you forgot. And that was the happiest and most important day of my life. It was the day I was introduced to you."

"Oh, Frank, I was beginning to feel terrible, thinking I had forgotten something really important, well, you know what I mean, like our engagement anniversary or the anniversary of our first date."

"Every little incident in my life with you is important, even after all these years."

"I think that is beautiful, Frank, that you preserve the tender memories of the little things and celebrate them with such thoughtful surprises," Joshua said.

"He's very thoughtful like that, Joshua. If anything, I'm the forgetful one," Sally said with a tinge of remorse in her expression.

At dinner the children were remarkably behaved; whether it was because of an awe they had for Joshua, or because they were ordinarily courteous and respectful, was hard to tell. They were not silent, but spoke in turn and were discreetly playful, like what Sarah had said to Joshua as they'd walked across the restaurant to their table.

"Joshua, you dropped something back there when we came in."

"I *did?* What did I drop?"

"Your footsteps."

"Well, in that case I will have to go back and pick them up."

"You can't do that," Sarah told him.

"No? Watch me."

Joshua rose from his chair, walked back across the restaurant, made as if he was picking something up from the floor, then returned to the table, seemingly holding something about the size of a shoe between his two hands.

"Here, Sarah, are my footprints."

"You can't pick up your footprints, silly."

"If I dropped them, I can. Here, take them," he said as he held them out to her.

Sarah reached out to take the footprints, and to her surprise, she could see nothing, but was holding something the shape of a sandal in her hands. She could feel it but could not see it.

"Joshua, how did you do that? I am really holding something," she said. "But now what do I do with it?"

"Anything you want. They are now yours. Bring them home with you."

"Daddy, look at this!"

"Look at what? I don't see anything. Joshua is just playing along with the trick you started," Frank said.

"No, no, Daddy. This really is real. Here, hold it if you don't believe me."

Her father reached out to accept whatever Sarah might give him. He, too, was just as shocked as Sarah.

"See, I told you."

Frank laughed.

"What is that, Joshua?" Frank asked.

"My footstep. It's my keepsake for Sarah, since she reminded me that I dropped it. And here is one for you, too, Carlie."

Carlie was too grown up for this kind of thing, and embarrassed, was reluctant to accept it, thinking it was all a joke.

"Well, I'll just put it down here near your place. When you leave you can take it with you. But when you get home, remember where you put them, otherwise you will have a hard time finding them."

"Oh, yeah," Carlie said, "because they're not real."

Sally was curious as to whether it was just a joke that everyone was going along with or whether there really was something there. So, she reached over and touched the footprint Joshua gave to Carlie.

"Carlie, it *is* real. Believe me, it *is* real."

"Not you, too, Mother."

During the meal, when no one else was watching, Carlie reached out and touched the footprint, then, in shock, screamed, "It *is* real, it *is* real. Joshua, how did you do that? Where am I going to keep it so I don't lose it. I will treasure it, but I can't tell anyone about it, because no one can see it."

"But they can touch it," Sarah said.

"Yeah, then what are you going to tell them, 'It's Joshua's footprint'? That's a likely story."

The three adults laughed at the dilemma the kids found themselves in.

They were halfway through the meal before they finally

settled the matter. Still they couldn't figure out what the "footprints" really were.

"Joshua," Frank said, turning to his guest, "Sally and I feel so foolish over our falling for that charlatan minister. I have to admit it was mostly my doing. Sally was reluctant to leave her job and bring the kids, but she trusted my judgment, and went along with me. I really called that one wrong. But what do you think about what's happening, with all the paranoia and anxiety?"

"Frank, people feel very insecure. The times are turbulent. The whole world is changing so radically, business is in turmoil, with companies going broke because their products are obsolete in a new version of the industrial revolution. People in the best years of their lives are losing their jobs with little hope of employment because of their age. As the earth seems to shrink people are exposed to all the chaos throughout the world, especially in countries where there is poverty and injustice. In simpler times, values were clearcut. Now people experience ways of life and moral attitudes they never dreamed of before, and they are frightened, for themselves, and even more for their children. When someone comes along and gives the illusion of having it all together, they flock to him because he promises a return to values people once treasured, and offers to create a new society based on people's dreams of an ideal community.

"Unfortunately, it is often too late before people realize that these leaders are deceivers, even of themselves."

"Joshua, we never realized how crazy the place was until the Leader told us, once we arrived there, that we would no

97

longer be responsible for teaching our own children. He had a specially trained staff who would be teaching them from then on. We immediately panicked, because we had already jealously guarded our children's education, and were very careful to know what they were being taught. There are so many bizarre and unhealthy values being passed off today as progressive and advanced, and state-of-the-culture so to speak, that we did not want people to be experimenting with our daughters. When we told the Leader that we insisted on teaching our own children, he freaked out. That was when we realized that we were dealing with a very unhealthy man. There was no hint of that when he came to our area and spoke here. He appeared so caring and so saintly that he immediately inspired trust in everyone. It was only when he had us committed and totally on his turf that he felt comfortable enough to act his true self. And what a revelation!

"But we were stuck there and, frankly, we were afraid to leave. We did not know how to go about it. We spent a lot of time planning what we could do, but were never sure, that is, until you came and so boldly burst into the dining hall and spoke your peace. You answered the prayers of so many of us that day. That was why such a large group left. They were all ready for the 'permission' you gave us, so, as soon as you finished speaking, we just got up and marched out. We would never have dared to do such a thing if you had not come and spoken to us. Again, we are most grateful, Joshua."

"I am glad you responded the way you did. I fear for those who did not respond, and pray they will listen to the gentle voice of the Spirit beckoning them to the freedom they surrendered when they went there. But I am concerned that many of them will not listen. If only they could foresee their fate!"

As they were leaving the restaurant, Joshua reminded the children not to forget their footsteps. Carlie had hers, but Sarah forgot where she put hers. She started crying, "Mommy, I can't find my footstep." As she looked all around for it the people at the nearby tables could not restrain their quiet laughter.

When she couldn't find it on the floor, Joshua went over and picked it up for her.

"Oh, thank you, Joshua. I hope I don't lose it again."

As the two girls walked out carrying their footsteps, everyone around was smiling at their beautiful simplicity. Little did they realize that those little girls had in their hands a most unique and treasured possession.

As soon as they got home, they devised a way to locate their footsteps to make sure they would never lose them again. They made little flags with a pole set in a round wooden base, and set them on top of each footstep, so they could see where they were. They did try gluing the base to the footstep but, for some reason, the glue would not stick.

By the time the children went to bed, Joshua had become their best friend, and they asked him if he would tell them a bedtime story, to which he readily agreed.

"When you are all ready to be tucked in, call me and I will tell you a bedtime story," he promised them as they went upstairs.

In no time at all, they called down to Joshua, "We're ready, Joshua. We're waiting for you."

Joshua walked up to their room and sat down in an old rocking chair next to the children's beds.

"Did you say good night to God?"

"Yes, we already did, Joshua. Now we're all ready for your story."

"Many, many years ago in a little village far away from here, there lived a little boy whose mother and father were sickly. The little boy was only ten years old. He couldn't go to school because he had to find jobs to earn money to take care of his ailing parents."

"What does ailing mean, Joshua?" Sarah asked.

"It means they were not well." He then continued, "The little boy's name was Michael because he was brave and unafraid. Michael would get up early every morning and try to find work. He would ask men in carpenter shops if they needed any help. Sometimes they would pay him to clean all the shavings off the floor. On other days he would help the mechanic who always needed help repairing cars. Now, Michael was too small to repair cars, but he was always willing to learn, and would run and get the tools when the mechanic needed them, and he would do all the menial work that the others did not like to do."

"What does 'menial' mean, Joshua?"

"Sarah, will you stop interrupting, you are ruining the story," Carlie said, annoyed.

"Menial means the lowly kind of work most people don't like to do."

"You mean like taking care of the garbage, and things like that?"

"Yes, Sarah. Now, Michael was not too proud to do

those menial things, so the chief mechanic liked him for that. He also was glad to have Michael run and get his tools when he needed them. The carpenter and the mechanic paid Michael enough money to care for his parents. They knew he was the only support of his mother and father. Michael also worked for other people when he had the time.

"Sometimes, however, when there was not much work to do, and Michael barely made enough money for food, he would buy food for his parents, and would make believe he had already eaten before he came home. Some days he would go without eating anything. On days when he earned extra money, he would also share what little he made with other people he knew were really poor, and were too sick to work.

"There were two young girls in the village whom Michael liked very much. One of the girls, whose name was Patricia, looked down on Michael because he was poor and did not wear nice clothes. Sometimes she would laugh at him in front of her friends. This hurt Michael very much. The other girl, whose name was Anna, could see more deeply into Michael's heart and saw how gentle and kind he was. Though she was embarrassed to talk to him, she secretly admired him, and would always ask people who knew Michael what he was like.

"Years later, Michael's mother and father died. Michael was eighteen years old then. By that time, he had a good job, but most of his money had been spent paying doctors to care for his sick parents. The two girls whom Michael liked still lived in the village. The one girl knew Michael liked her, but for some strange reason, she was always mean to him, humbling him in front of her friends. She did not want anyone to think that she could like someone poor. Michael could not understand why she was so cruel, because he was always courteous and proper toward her. The other girl, however, though she was not very pretty, was kind and Michael could see goodness radiating from her, especially when she smiled. When she laughed, it was infectious, and everyone around her would laugh, too. Everyone enjoyed being near her because she made them happy, and made them feel good about themselves.

"Living in the vicinity was a very wealthy man, who owned a vast estate and great investments, but he and his wife could never have any children. As the man grew old, he wondered what he should do with all his great wealth. His wife suggested to him one day that he entrust his wealth to someone who would administer it wisely. But who? The wife told her husband all about Michael, and how he'd cared for his sick parents ever since he was a young boy, and how on Sundays she would see him in church, always praying with his head down, deep in thought, so remarkable for a lad his age.

"The man thought and thought for the longest time, then decided that his wife's suggestion might be a good idea, but the young man would have to be taught how to administer all his wealth wisely. He sent for Michael and asked if he would be willing to help him with his work, and be an assistant to him. Over the years, Michael and the old man became the best of friends, while the old man taught him all about his vast possessions. Never did Michael dream what the man had in mind, and when the day came for the old man to tell Michael of his plans, Michael could not believe it, and was reluctant to accept. But when the old man explained how important it was and how many people he could help with the great power his possessions would give him, Michael accepted.

"By that time, Michael had married the girl who was kind to him. It was a splendid wedding. The old man was so proud of his 'adopted' son. The party lasted for three days, and was held at the old man's estate. The other girl whom Michael liked had also married by that time. She and her husband were invited to the wedding. They were shocked to see the splendor in which the 'poor' boy now lived, and the vast wealth at his disposal.

"Not long afterward, the old man died, followed shortly by his wife. Michael was now in charge of all of the old man's possessions. In good times and in bad times, Michael prospered. The kindness he had shown in his childhood showed even more wonderfully now that he could share his great wealth with those who were suffering hard times. The girl who had been unkind to Michael had also gone through bad times. She and her husband had been reduced to poverty. When this came to Michael's attention, not wanting to embarrass her, he asked his wife to quietly help them so they could live with a certain level of dignity. The positions Michael's wife arranged for them were in one of Michael's businesses, which brought them in contact with Michael whenever he came to visit the officials in charge. They were shocked when they found out that Michael owned even the extensive business in which they were employed. But Michael was always kind to them when he met them, and always treated them with dignity and respect. He made them feel proud that they were doing such good work. In her heart, the woman thought so many times, 'If I was kind to him when we were young, I would now be his wife and not just a worker in one of his businesses.' "

"Joshua, I think Sarah fell asleep," Carlie said, "but she heard most of the story. I was so excited to find out what happened, I couldn't wait to hear the ending. That was an awesome story, Joshua. Thank you so much. I'll tell Sarah how it ended tomorrow morning. Good night. I love you, Joshua."

"I love you, too, Carlie. May my Father bless you and Sarah, even in your sleep, and send your guardian angels to watch over you."

JOSHUA SPENT THE next two days walking through the city, meeting people along the way, and as in days of long ago, stopping to chat with strangers, and anyone relaxed enough to spend a few minutes talking with him.

It was not difficult for Joshua to involve someone in a conversation. He had the rare knack of piquing a person's curiosity by asking a simple question, such as, "Why are people so anxious over the year two thousand?" or, "Ma'am, I can see you are deep in thought. Why do you worry so much about your son? He will be all right. His heavenly Father watches over him day and night. He will pass through these difficult times. Just pray hard for him and trust."

Though people are not as casual and relaxed on modern city streets as they were in times past, there are still those who feel free enough to talk to a stranger and not think it odd. Joshua, of course, knew all about people before he approached them. Usually, it was someone troubled about family or the harshness of life. The question Joshua would ask people was just what they were thinking at that moment. Shocked at his insight, they were spontaneously drawn into conversation with him.

Walking down the street in the business area, he came across a man passing out pamphlets about the end of the world. The man must have been standing there a long time, because he was shifting from one foot to another in an attempt to keep warm.

"Young man, are these your writings?" Joshua asked him.

"No, sir. I am distributing them for the organization I work with. They are experts in the Bible, and teach the end of the world coming very soon. We have been asked to hand out these pamphlets to alert those who are 'chosen by God' about the terrible times to come."

"Olaf, do you believe there are terrible times to come?"

"I don't know, sir. I just do as I am told. I don't know anything about these things. Sir, you know my name?"

"Yes, I have always known you."

"I'm sorry, sir, but you're kind of making me nervous. You sound sort of creepy."

"There is no need to be nervous. My Father shares many things with me, and I listen to his word."

"You speak like Jesus speaks in the gospels. Do you know about the end of the world coming?"

"Do not worry about the end of the world. My Father's creation will not come to an end until it is perfected. That will take a long, long time. There is still much work to do. My Father wants His children to be happy. He does not want them to be anxious and worried about His coming. That makes Him look like a monster of some sort. The only end of the world people should be concerned about, and indeed, they should look forward to it, is the moment when their life here on earth comes to an end, and my Father calls them home. That should be a happy time, not filled with fear and anxiety."

"You mean I shouldn't be passing these things out?"

"That is right. It does no honor to my Father to make people frightened of Him when He wants them to look upon Him as a loving Father."

"Do you mean I don't have to be afraid of God?"

"That's right, Olaf. God knows you from your first moment. He knows you make mistakes that you feel bad about. He understands. He knows you don't want to do bad things. He also knows you try to be good. My Father loves you, just as you are. You never have to worry about Him loving you. He watches over and protects you every moment of each day. So, just rest in His love and when you walk the streets, feeling so alone, know that you are not really alone. God is with you, by your side, as your friend."

"Gee, mister, thank you. What is your name?"

"Joshua."

"Joshua, that's a nice name. The Bible teacher said that that was Jesus' name in Hebrew."

"Yes, that is my name."

"You're sort of like Jesus then, aren't you?"

"Yes, and I'm your friend."

"Thanks, Joshua. But what am I going to do for food now? They were paying me to pass out these things; not much, but just enough for food."

"Two blocks down the street, there is a very old man selling papers. He knows he cannot do it much longer, but can't afford to give up. Go down and help him. He will be very grateful. It will give him a chance to go home early each day and rest. He lives in a little old house not far from there. He will invite you to come and stay with him, if you are willing to help him each day. So, Olaf, you see, you never have to worry. Your Father watches over you always."

The man thanked Joshua, threw the pamphlets into a barrel, and almost ran down the street to meet the old man, so excited was he at the prospect of a new life, simple as it was, opening before him.

Joshua looked after him, smiling.

While Joshua walked the streets meeting people, Sally was busy promoting the interview. Two days of spot announcements at the most popular times of the day and night assured a vast audience.

When the time came, Frank drove Joshua to the studio. Joshua was a little taken aback when a girl came in with makeup and asked if he minded.

"You mean you don't like me the way I am?" he said with half a smile.

"No, it's not that, sir. It's just that we have to make

sure the bright lights won't reflect off shiny spots on your face."

Sally came in at that point. "Oh, Joshua getting makeup! Somehow, I can't think of you with makeup."

"Don't spoil it, Sally. I just got him to let me to put it on," the makeup girl said, slightly annoyed.

"Well, Joshua, are you ready for your interview?"

"I am looking forward to it."

"In five minutes we start."

Finished with his makeup, he followed Sally into the studio, where he was escorted to his place on the set, and hooked up to a microphone. Sally took her place on the opposite side of a coffee table set between them.

"This evening we are indeed honored and privileged to have a most extraordinary guest with us. His name is Joshua, just plain Joshua. I could get no other name from him. Any of you who were downtown this afternoon may have seen our guest wandering along Main Street talking to people. I doubt if anyone would have taken notice of him, or paid any attention to him, so ordinary and unassuming are his appearance and manner. The first time I saw him, I was unimpressed until he began to speak. We were at the commune I told you about not too long ago. Joshua bravely came into the dining room where we were gathered, and began to speak about the life to which we had just committed ourselves. We were all, at that point, beginning to feel uncomfortable about this new life, and where it might eventually lead us. The more discerning among us were witnessing attitudes and restrictions that were whittling away at our freedom and self-respect. But we were afraid to do anything about it. Any questioning of the Leader drew down upon us a mountain of guilt.

"Then, Joshua seemed to have just appeared out of nowhere, and began speaking to the whole assembly about the frightful dangers inherent in what we were doing. The leaders were horrified, but for some unexplainable reason no response from them was forthcoming. They just sat there dumb. After Joshua's talk, literally a third of the group picked up their belongings and left the commune. It turned out to be our salvation.

"Joshua, I can never be grateful enough for what you have done for us. Now, we have you here in our studio. Tell us a little about yourself! What do you do? Where do you live?"

"I am just myself. Like St. Francis of long ago, I just wander from place to place getting to know people and sharing with them my vision of life."

"Joshua, you are too humble. You are much more than that. That older man you were staying with up in the mountains had almost a kind of veneration for you. He obviously knew something about you the rest of us would give anything to know."

"Perhaps it is that I am so simple."

"Well, since you are so modest about yourself, let me ask you some questions. You have unique views about the millennium, a subject about which half the world is concerned. Many are afraid that the end of the world may be approaching. What do you think? Would you share with our audience some of your ideas?"

"There is no basis for people's fear of the world coming to an end. God doesn't do things violently like that, nor does He want people to live in fear or on the edge of terror. He created His children to be happy, and religious leaders who frighten people over impending doom do not understand Jesus' message. Jesus came to free people from that kind of fear."

"What about the new millennium?"

"My Father does not follow people's calendar. If He decides to bring the world to an end, it will be when the work of His creation is perfected. When all things are brought together in God's Son, then will creation be perfected. There is still much work to be done. Much work. If the world is destroyed before then, it will be the doing of perverse human minds, not the work of my Father. Massive destructive weapons to kill God's children are the things you should fear. They are capable of destroying my Father's creation before its time. People must learn to live simple lives again, and learn to care for one another and forgive. Unforgiveness is the greatest danger to humanity, and the most virulent evil on earth. It is becoming so widespread, it can ultimately destroy the whole human race."

"But there are many clergy who will not agree with you. They say that the scriptures point to our times as the time when the world will come to an end."

"Nowhere does it say that in the scriptures. Passages they use refer to times and situations long past. Jesus warned His followers not to listen to those kinds of false prophets. They lead the people astray. The only end that people must be concerned about is the moment when God takes them out of this world, the time of their death. That is all that should concern them. It is the moment they will meet God. For those who love God and care for others, they need not be afraid. Only people who live for themselves and are filled with hatred and unforgiveness need fear the end of their life."

"When you visited that commune up in the mountains, Joshua, what was it that concerned you?"

"Sally, that is not the only place where people are being led astray. But that place is the work of the devil. I grieve for the people who chose to stay, because horrible things will befall them soon, and they are not willing to listen to those who would reach out to help them."

"But, Joshua, how can we tell who is a good religious leader and who is leading people astray? It is so difficult for us. I know, and I am now embarrassed over it, we were led astray by that man until you helped us to see the light."

"By their fruits you shall know them. If they love God and teach goodness and love and understanding of others, they are good shepherds. If they teach fear and hatred and suspicion of others, and constantly focus people's attention on the devil, they are doing the work of the devil and giving Satan the prominent place in people's minds and the attention Satan is looking for. When people's attention and love are focused on Jesus, they need not fear Satan, because their hearts are filled with God. It is only hearts devoid of love that provide breeding ground for Satan's legions."

"Joshua, ministers point out that wars and ominous changes in weather patterns and natural disasters are signs that God is preparing punishment for this evil generation. Do you think this is true?"

"Tell me a time when there were no wars, and frightening changes in nature, and violent upheavals. These times are no different than any other times. There have been evil people all throughout history. But no matter how much evil there is, there are so many good people, struggling to create a better world, why would my Father want to punish them? My Father is not dismayed by evil. Remember, He created human beings, and is well aware of how flawed they are. He has infinite patience with even the most selfish. Why do people think that God is always looking for a chance to punish and inflict calamity on His children? This is the farthest thing from my Father's mind. It doesn't even make sense. Remember, He is a God of love, not a God of violence.

"This year there will be natural disasters, frightening tragedies, and not only in far away countries. But these things happen in the natural course of events. People must not see the hand of a punishing God in them, and should just get on with their lives. Scientists have given people many warnings, and they should heed those warnings. Scientists, just like theologians, help people to understand God and His creation. Science also teaches about God, and about how God created this world. People should learn from science. God cannot contradict in His revelation what He has placed in His creation. What scientists find in creation should help people understand better what the Spirit has revealed in scripture."

"Joshua, you just remarked that there would be natural

disasters 'not only in far away countries.' What did you mean by that?"

"This country, as beautiful as it is and as good as its people are, is still part of the planet, which is forever changing. People who live in fragile places should heed the warnings of scientists. It is not wise to take risks in matters so important."

"Joshua, you are still not precise. I sense you know something about the future that you are unwilling to spell out in more detail. I will respect your reserve on this matter. But I would like to suggest to our audience that this man's advice should not be easily shrugged off. Now, Joshua, an important question. People seem to be seriously searching for a meaning to their lives, and for personal spirituality, but they also seem to be drifting away from the churches. Doesn't that seem to be paradoxical?"

"No, people will always hunger for intimacy with God. When churches fail to teach people how to draw near to God, which is their prime responsibility, people will look for God on their own and develop their own substitutes for religion. Then the churches, rather than listen to the silent cries of the people for guidance, attack their feeble attempts to find meaning to life outside of church. The churches have to begin focusing on God again, and on people's need for God, and like the mystics of the past, teach people how to develop intimacy with God. The Church has all this wisdom, but clergy spend little time developing people's spirituality. That is why the people are drifting away from church."

"Do you think church is necessary?"

"Of course it is. Church is nothing more than God's

children gathering together as a family to worship God, and pray for one another. My Father is pleased when He sees His children praying and worshiping as a family. But when they come together it is important that His shepherds feed the sheep and not send them away hungry. Otherwise they force them to look for nourishment elsewhere. It is then that the sheep wander into dangerous places and get lost. This is why the Good Shepherd is always going out in search for the lost and hurting sheep."

"Joshua, you bring tears to my eyes. Are you that Good Shepherd?"

"Sally, *you* have said it. The Good Shepherd will always wander through the world looking for the bruised and hurting sheep. The Good Shepherd's love for the sheep is very tender, and does not wish that even one sheep be lost."

"Joshua, thank you for being on our show this evening. It has been indeed an honor for me to have had this chance to interview you."

"Thank you, Sally, for this wonderful chance to speak to the people. You made it very enjoyable."

"This is Sally Blair for Channel 10 and 'New Perspectives.' Thank you for listening and good night."

Afterward in Sally's office, the camera crew came in to meet Joshua personally. Joshua's interview shook up everyone. They all had questions. They had never heard anyone speak so frankly and knowledgeably about those issues.

"Joshua," Sally asked him, "can I ask you privately and off the record what you meant when you were hinting at natural disasters not far away?"

"People who live in those areas know. They have been

warned for years by seismologists that something catastrophic will take place in the not too distant future. No one heeds their warnings."

"Can you be specific?"

Smiling, Joshua answered, "Sally, you know where I mean. It is at this moment on your mind."

"Joshua, don't tell me you can read my mind, too. Oh no. Now I'm embarrassed."

"Don't be."

"That was the question I wanted to ask as well," said one of the camera crew. "Sally, I guess I'll have to ask you. Sally, what place were you thinking about?"

"California," she answered.

Joshua smiled, but said nothing as they all looked at him for acknowledgment.

"Joshua," Sally said, "I am very pleased with the interview. Judging by the notes on my desk here, other stations have already called and want to use it on their local channels. I wouldn't be surprised if it becomes nationally syndicated."

"People need guidance during these difficult times," Joshua replied.

"I'll be ready in a few minutes if you can wait, Joshua. I'll drive you to the house and we can have something to eat. I'm sure Frank will want to quiz you about the interview."

On the way to the house, Sally unexpectedly started to cry.

"What is it, Sally?" Joshua asked.

"I'm sorry—it's just that I can't stop worrying about my sister. She and her husband are having difficult problems and I am at my wit's end trying to help them. I was wondering if you could talk to them. I know you are not married, but you have such insight into people's hearts, I was hoping you might give them some advice."

"I would be happy to."

"They will probably be at the house when we get there. I know they want to meet you. If the two of them are open to it, you might talk to them in the den where it is quiet. If you don't mind."

When Sally and Joshua entered the house, Carlie and Sarah met them at the door, and each grabbed Joshua's hand. He bent down and hugged them.

In the living room, Frank and Sally's sister, Jane, and her husband Mike, were having hors d'oeuvres before supper. They all arose when Joshua entered.

"Enter our celebrity!" Frank said, as Joshua and Sally entered.

Joshua blushed.

"That was quite an interview," Frank said. "For your first time on television, you had the poise and presence of a professional. And you said some really powerful things. I don't expect everybody will agree with you, but they are things I have never heard anyone say before. I hope they are well received, especially by the clergy."

"Thank you, Frank."

"This is my sister, Jane, Joshua. And this is her husband, Mike."

They all reached out to shake hands.

"I can't tell you how happy we are to have this chance to meet you, Joshua," Jane said.

"Joshua, would you like something to drink?" Frank asked.

"Yes, that would really be nice after that grueling interview," Joshua answered jokingly. "Does Sally interrogate *you* like that, Frank?"

Laughing, Frank responded, "You think that was bad; you got away easy compared to what I go through."

"Oh, you guys! You poor babies, afraid of a little lady asking you a few innocent questions!"

"Sally, you never asked an innocent question in your life," Frank retorted with a broad grin.

"Well, that's my field of expertise. How else am I going to get the answers I'm looking for? Let's sit down for this wonderful dinner Frank has prepared for us. Who ever thought a man could cook such a delicious meal?"

The children insisted on sitting next to Joshua, so they sat on either side of him, much to his pleasure.

"Carlie, it's your turn to say the grace," Sally reminded her.

"Dear God, thank you for everything. Thank you for sending Jesus at Christmas. Thank you for Mommy and Daddy, and especially for Joshua. Thank you for Aunt Jane and Uncle Mike, and also for Sarah. And please bless this nice supper Daddy cooked, but please let Mommy cook next time."

"And I thought you were my friend, Carlie," Frank said.

"I am, Daddy. You're my best friend, but Mommy is my

best cook. You cook what big people like. Mommy cooks what I like."

After the meal Jane asked Joshua if she and her husband could talk with him for a few minutes. The three of them excused themselves and walked into the den.

"You look like a very happy couple," Joshua said to open the conversation.

"Oh, we are," Jane responded, "but we have been going through some really rough times lately, and we don't know how to get past them. I thought you would be helpful if we could talk to you, since, from what my sister said, you are so understanding."

"What is it that is troubling you?" Joshua asked.

"Mike is spending more and more time at work, and I'm left home alone with the three children. I try to talk to him about it, but he won't discuss it. I think he's falling out of love with me, and I feel horrible. I don't know what to do about it."

"Do you love your wife, Mike?" Joshua asked matter-of-factly, catching Mike completely off guard.

"I've never stopped loving her, but there are so many pressures now, that I have to spend more time at work."

"I have a feeling that is not the real reason, Mike. Look inside yourself and give me the real reason."

"Joshua, I'm not a crybaby. I don't like complaining. When life gets difficult, I make the best of it without complaining."

"That's still not an answer, Mike. What is it that you don't like complaining about? Obviously, something is troubling you, and you're keeping it inside."

"Jane is a good mother, Joshua. And I am very grateful she does such a good job with the kids."

"Why do you emphasize she is such a good mother, and not mention that she's a good wife?"

"Joshua, you're a tricky one. She *is* a good wife. She is very thoughtful and faithful to all her responsibilities."

"But you are holding back. What is it that you feel is lacking?"

"Joshua, you'd make a good chess player. You keep pushing and pushing until you checkmate. Well, I am not complaining, but ever since the kids have come along, they take up all Jane's time and there is little time left for us. At night she is too tired to even spend a few quiet minutes together without falling asleep or complaining of a headache. I feel she doesn't need me anymore, so rather than complain about it, I throw myself into my work and spend more time at the office. We can use the extra money anyway. Before we know it, the kids will be going to college, and we have to have the money for that. That's why I spend all the time at the office."

"Well, Jane, what do you think of that?"

"I don't think I spend that much time with the children. That's just an excuse."

"To Mike it seems to be quite important. To say it is just an excuse is telling him you don't believe what he feels. Why, then, should he express what he feels if you do not believe him? There is no place to go from there, except silence, and not say what he feels. What Mike is saying is a very common problem that sometimes people do not like to face. What Mike is saying is that he feels you used to enjoy spend-

120

ing more time with him, and you both enjoyed that special time. When was the last occasion you spent some special time together?"

There was silence, broken after a brief pause, as Jane continued, "But the children take up so much time. When do we have a free minute from them? From the minute they get up in the morning until the time they go to bed at night, they are constantly needing something."

"Isn't it nice to know that they need you?"

"Yes, of course."

"And when you don't pay attention to them, what do they do?"

"They get hurt and complain and start whining."

"And what do big children do when their needs are not being met?"

"They stay busy and work late, so they don't have to act like children and whine," Jane said, laughing, as she looked at Mike, who was smiling at Joshua's clever maneuvering.

"So, you see. You both love each other deeply, and if that is your only problem, you are blessed. Be sensitive to each other's needs. And, Mike, you could spend more time with the children yourself, so Jane wouldn't have to be with them all the time. Marriage is a partnership, and it works best when the burdens are shared. If Jane can get some time to herself and spend some time with her friends, you will be surprised how much more she will enjoy spending time with you."

"Thanks, Joshua," they both said together. "You've been a big help."

After saying good-bye to the rest of the family, Mike and Jane left for home.

"How did it go, Joshua?" Sally asked.

"They are just fine. You won't have to worry about them. They are very much in love."

"Thanks, Joshua. Now, after this long day, I think we all need a good rest. That *was* a good supper, Frank, in spite of what Carlie said about your cooking."

"She has a subtle sense of humor for such a little child," Frank responded. "She is so lovable."

CHAPTER 9

THE NEXT MORNING Joshua left the Blairs, much to the children's sorrow, though he promised to be never far away from them, and never to forget them. Those few days created memories the family would treasure for the rest of their lives. His leaving, however, left them with many questions. When asked if they could drop him off at the bus stop or at the train station, he declined. As it was snowing heavily, they felt bad seeing him walk out into such miserable weather, but he said he enjoyed walking in the snow.

They watched him for the longest time as he walked down the driveway. At one point, he just disappeared. They debated among themselves as to whether the heavy snow hid him from sight or if he had just disappeared. The children, who were watching him closely, said that he did not gradually fade from sight in the snow, but that all of a sudden he wasn't there. They all wondered who this man was who could read their thoughts, understand the workings of the human mind and emotions with such depth, and have such boundless love and concern for people, even strangers. Was he just a stranger passing through, or was he something more, come among us to guide a world that had lost its way?

THE FOLLOWING DAY, Sally received a phone call from Atlanta, Georgia. It was a producer at CNN who had seen her interview of Joshua, and was asking if he could meet with Joshua for an in-depth discussion of issues. "This guy's got it all together," he told her, "and he's not afraid to talk." Sally could give him no information, other than that she was sure he would be showing up in other places around the country, and suggested the producer give the word to CNN's local affiliates to keep an eye out for him.

Joshua did reappear, and that is the only word to describe his comings and goings, as reappearances. It was early spring, and it was on the outskirts of Denver, Colorado, at a quiet retreat where young people spent time away from home, to work at their jobs or attend college, and study scripture. The director, Bob Krulish, was working outside when he saw a stranger walking up the driveway, walking as if he knew where he was going.

"Can I help you?" Bob said, in his open, friendly manner.

"I hope so. My name is Joshua. I was hoping I could spend some time here with you and your little family."

Being a man of deep faith, it did not take Bob long to sense that, in this poorly dressed stranger, there was more than just a wandering beggar.

"Yes, by all means. You are most welcome. In fact, it's almost time for supper, and if you haven't eaten yet, you are welcome to eat here with us."

Bringing the stranger inside, he led him upstairs to a room facing the front of the house. On the door was a little card, which had been put there for a previous guest, and which read, "Welcome, Joshua!" They both laughed when they saw it.

"How timely!" Bob said. "I might as well leave it there."

The two men sat down and talked. Joshua seemed to Bob to be a friendly enough fellow, the type who sets you right at ease, and whom you instinctively know you can trust.

"Where are you from?" Bob asked him.

"I'm just wandering around. I don't need money, so I travel from place to place to meet people and spread the message of God's goodness, helping them to realize they don't have to spend half their life wondering what life is all about."

"What is life all about?"

"It is very simple. God created this vast universe, placed His children in the middle of it to solve its riddles and enjoy its wonders, and to care for one another, and then, when they die, go home and live with Him, and all their loved ones."

"Profound, and so simple. Well, why don't you wash up, take a shower if you like, everything's there, and, when you finish, come down and we'll all have supper."

"Thank you, Bob."

On his way down the stairs, Bob scratched his head, thinking, "I don't remember telling him my name. I asked him his, but I didn't tell him mine. How did he know?"

Gathering for supper were a half dozen young people, between nineteen and twenty-six. They were open and friendly. Each of them carried with them his or her pain and experiences from the past. They were still trying to sort it all out and find meaning to their lives, if there was one. They had heard from friends about the existence of this place of retreat. It was a place where they could work at their jobs or college classes, and in the evenings, after supper, gather for informal discussions about the Bible, and share with one another personal problems.

When Joshua entered the kitchen, they were all standing around chatting.

"You're Joshua, we know you already. Welcome to our home! I'm Jessica, this is Jane, Tom, Harry, Jennifer, Maria, and Mike."

"I am happy to meet all of you. I hope I get a chance to know more about each of you, if you are not too busy."

"We're all laid back here. You came at a good time. We're pretty free on the weekends, so we'll be seeing a lot of each other," Jane said.

"Whatever you're having for supper, it smells good," Joshua commented.

"Food's always good here," said Tom.

As they were talking, Bob entered.

"Well, here comes our fearless leader. Now we can all sit down to supper," Mike remarked.

Joshua walked into the dining room and immediately sat at the foot of the table. When everyone was seated, they bowed their heads and Bob offered grace.

"Well, I guess you all met our new guest," Bob said. "I'm looking forward to getting to know you, Joshua."

"I feel welcome already. You are all so warm and cordial. Thank you."

"Where is home?" Jane asked.

"Wherever I am," Joshua replied.

"Any place permanent?" she continued.

"Lately, each day it's different."

"Where were you last, if I am not prying?"

"Ohio."

"Anything interesting happen there?" she pressed further.

"Spent time with a wonderful family. The mother was anchor woman for the television station, and asked if I would do an interview with her."

Everyone's eyes turned toward Joshua, as if wondering, "Why would anyone want to do an interview with him—he's just a homeless wanderer."

"May I ask what the interview was about?" Jessica asked.

"It was about the subject that is on so many people's minds, the end of the millennium."

"Why did the lady interview you?" Jessica persisted.

"She and a group of other people had had a frightening experience with a religious commune, and I was able to help them. They were grateful. When they returned home, and I was in their area, the woman asked if I would appear on her program."

"Weren't you nervous?" Bob asked.

"Not at all. I feel very comfortable with people."

"What happened at the commune?"

"Their Leader is a very misguided individual and has serious personal problems, which I saw would bring tragedy upon the whole group. I spoke to them one day and a large number of them left and went back to their homes and families. The people from Ohio were among them."

"Wasn't their Leader upset with what you did?" she continued.

"Yes."

"Joshua," Bob said, "you haven't touched your food yet. Why don't we give Joshua a chance to eat first, then we can all get acquainted afterward."

After supper, they invited their friends Jerry and Martha Dell Lewis for dessert. The house they were all staying in had once been the Lewis' home. They donated it for use by young people as a place for prayer and healing, and leadership training. Ever since, hundreds of young people had benefited from their generosity and their friendship.

The drawing room was large, but carefully furnished to preserve a warm, homey atmosphere. The gently falling snow outside added to the charm of the evening in the softly lighted room.

"Joshua, this is Jerry and Martha Dell. They are our sponsors and dear friends," Bob said as he introduced them.

"They are blessed to have such caring friends," Joshua said to the couple as they hugged him.

"Welcome to our little family," Jerry responded.

They all sat down to indulge in ice cream topped with plum sauce, which the cook made especially for the evening.

"Bob called and told me you had come to visit. It is nice to have you, Joshua," Martha Dell said, as her way of welcoming the stranger, but then there were no strangers at this house. Everyone was treated as a guest, in honor of the Special Guest who might some day come unannounced. One could never tell when this Visitor, in humble, unassuming form, might present himself without fanfare to unsuspecting hosts. Fortunate are the rare ones who can see Goodness beneath the trappings of a poor beggar, for only they will be wise enough to entertain with dignity divinity clothed in humble attire.

Though these simple people had no idea who was visiting this evening, they could not have treated royalty with more affable consideration.

"How do you like our part of the country, Joshua?" Jerry asked.

"It is so beautiful, reflecting in rare fashion the majesty of God's greatness. Though even here I see signs of neglect for this extraordinary natural treasure. The sky at one time was so pure and blue, but unhealthy colors now mar its purity. My Father has entrusted His magnificent universe to His children. It is so important they treat every plant and animal, as well as the earth and water, as precious gifts. It is *their* children's inheritance."

"Joshua, you strike me as being very much in tune with people and with nature," Martha said to him. "How did you come about this remarkable ability?"

"I see everything as a little child would and have never lost my sense of wonder. It is as fresh today as it was from the very beginning. I look across creation each day, and see that it is good. The balance in creation is a vivid evidence of God's genius. Preserving that balance He has entrusted to you, and all His children. That demands much love and care."

"What brings you up our way?" Bob asked him.

"There are things I must do, and people about whom I am concerned. You live in difficult times, times and circumstances that many people cannot comprehend and resolve. Human intelligence has crafted inventions that are beyond its ability to control. That is dangerous."

"Do you think you can help?" Mike asked.

"In some ways I can, by helping people appreciate values they have cast aside as simplistic or old-fashioned. Fear, distrust, and need to outperform the accomplishments of others have inspired many of today's inventions. This has generated unhealthy competition and false patriotism, and made enemies where there were no enemies. Good inventions then become weapons that people use in everyday life, to hurt, humiliate, or destroy others. Love, understanding, and forgiveness are being replaced by mean competition. This has to change if people are to survive. What you young men and women do here is a good first step."

It was late when the group retired. Jerry and Martha Dell invited Joshua for a tour of the area the next day. He was grateful and looked forward to it.

With the change in atmosphere and thinness of the mountain air Joshua slept soundly. The next morning, he awoke to bright sunshine and fresh crisp air. What a beautiful place to live was his first thought.

Breakfast was hectic, as people had to leave for work or class. Each ate at his or her convenience. Joshua sat and talked with the cook while eating the bacon and eggs she had prepared for him. As he finished, Bob and his wife, Judy, entered and took Joshua for a stroll around the grounds. They were well kept by the guests and there were quiet places when someone needed space to be alone.

Walking near the tiny chapel, Bob pointed out a stone memorial to their son, who had died. They stood for a few minutes meditating, and offering a prayer.

"He is now blessed. If you could see the joy and friendships that fill his life, it would lessen your pain. He is now his perfect self, and each of his days is filled with friends and ever new, exciting experiences. And he is never far from you at any moment, so talk to him when you think of him. He hears and understands. Your prayers deepen his joy in heaven."

They both thanked Joshua for his comforting insights.

At that point Jerry arrived to pick up Joshua for their sight-seeing tour, though it was more for a chance to talk rather than see sights. Jerry had at one time owned the largest private oil company in the country, and initiated the development of Vail, and though still in the business, he and Martha Dell spent much of their life being "father" and "mother" to many searching young people.

The sight-seeing was not in the city, where there were myriad attractions, but out in the mountains, where the views were breathtaking and the air crisp and clear. They did the strenuous hike up to Bierstadt Lake, named after the famous painter. The lake is like a jewel set in a hollow of the mountain, a quiet, peaceful setting. Even though Joshua was familiar with everything he saw, the actual experience of seeing was overwhelming to him, and, after brushing the snow from a log lying on the ground next to him, he sat and drank in the scene for the longest time. Jerry was impressed with his unusual ability to concentrate.

"Well, Joshua," Jerry said after waiting for him to finish his meditation, "shall we continue with our sight-seeing?"

On the way to Georgetown, the old mining village, they talked. Jerry was curious to learn more about Joshua, and Joshua was interested in involving Jerry in work that had to be done.

"Joshua, I watch you when you talk. You give me the impression you know what a person is going to say even before he opens his mouth. Why do I sense that?"

Joshua laughed. "Jerry, suppose I tell you that I just know?"

"I wouldn't be shocked, but then I suppose it would be more discreet at that point if I just respected your privacy, and not pried any further. But I do have other questions. For example, what are your ideas on religion? Do you feel church is necessary?"

"Church is nothing more than people gathering together to pray. Of course, that *is* necessary if people are going to be the family God intended. God is not pleased when people cut themselves off from others and tell God they will worship Him on their own, and in the way they want. Jesus gathered people together in community, and promised to be forever with the apostles he appointed to lead that community. So, church, as people now call it, is important, and the apostles he sent are still here to teach and guide. Accepting them is also important, if people are to honor God in the way He directed."

"Does anybody ever really do that?"

"No one does it perfectly, but God has always accepted people's far less than perfect attempts to do what is right."

"How can we understand what God is trying to teach us by reading the Bible?"

"Jerry, Jesus never gave people a book. He gave teachers and sent to them the Holy Spirit to guide them to an ever-deepening understanding of his message. Jesus has kept his promise and has been guiding the Church for two thousand years. Its understanding of Jesus' message and the written word is much more authentic than the thoughts of people who just pick up the Bible and study it. There is a two-thousand-year-old memory in the Church formed by the Holy Spirit to guarantee the faithful transmission of Jesus' message until the end of time. Since Jesus required acceptance of his message for entrance into God's kingdom, he had to ensure its integrity forever. And to this day that living message continues in spite of the personal lives of the apostles' descendants, and cannot be rejected if people intend to be loyal to Jesus."

"Joshua, that's a heavy dose. I don't know whether I could accept it all. I admit it's logical, but the Church has gone in so many different directions and there are many good people in each of the churches."

"That is true, and God understands the struggle people have in trying to do the right thing, and judges them on their sincerity. But the integrity of Jesus' message is of prime importance; otherwise Jesus wasted his time in coming to earth. His message has been fragmented and twisted in a thousand different ways. That does not please God. God's mind is one and His message has to have unity to give proper guidance to people. It cannot be taught in ways that are contradictory. That is why before he died, Jesus prayed to His Father that his disciples "would be one, even as you and I are one, so that people may believe that you have sent me." He foresaw what would happen, and prayed that that division would be healed, so his family could be united in belief and love. It is not right for God's family to be divided and estranged from one another. I know it will take time, but leaders have to persistently work toward unity if they are to be faithful to Jesus. The community Jesus began still exists, and people must open their hearts to understand and appreciate it. It will always be present as a light in darkness until the end of time. Jesus promised that. Men cannot appoint themselves as apostles. They must be chosen by apostles before them. Otherwise, like branches broken off the vine, they and their followers will eventually wither and die."

By now they were approaching Georgetown, which had very little life in the middle of winter. The townsfolk were friendly and the people in the tiny bookstore were most cordial in their welcome, offering Jerry and Joshua hot mulled cider, which Joshua had never tasted before and raved over. Jerry treated Joshua to early supper, then they started on their way back to the city.

"Jerry, thank you so much for a wonderful afternoon. If you are not busy tomorrow, would I be imposing if I asked you to drive me up into the mountain to visit a group of people who are in desperate need of help?"

"No, not at all. What time would you like to go?"

"After breakfast would be a good time, if that is convenient. And I think Martha Dell would also enjoy this little venture."

"Okay, I'll see if she is going to be free. Thank you, too, Joshua. I enjoyed spending this time with you. It was a rare treat. Your dress and demeanor belie the person you really are. You are not just the simple fellow you like people to think you are," Jerry said with a twinkle in his eye.

Joshua laughed, but said nothing.

"So, tomorrow at nine o'clock sharp," Jerry said as he dropped Joshua off at the house.

"Have a peaceful evening and again, thank you, Jerry," Joshua said as he closed the car door.

Joshua dreamed that night. He dreamed of a world renewed, a world as his Father once dreamed it, a world of great spiritual and material prosperity where happiness and peace prevailed, and where each individual found true fulfillment and joy in doing the work he or she was destined to accomplish. But upon waking, the dream turned to depression as he realized he was still in the real world made so frightening by the selfishness of many.

During breakfast, Joshua invited the cook to sit and chat with him. She told him about her family and about her life. Joshua listened attentively and told her God had picked her to do a special work, and that each day she touched the lives of the young people who had come there searching. One day she would see all the wonderful things God was able to accomplish through her kind and thoughtful ways.

Jerry and Martha Dell arrived precisely on time. Joshua was waiting at the door.

"Well, hop in, young man! Your friend was delighted to be able to come with us today. I don't think she knows what she's in for."

"Good morning, Joshua!"

"Good morning, Martha Dell. I am glad you were free to come with us. I think you will have a good time."

"I'm sure I will."

"Well, Joshua, you're going to have to tell me where to go, as I don't have the slightest idea," Jerry said. "First of all, do you know where this place is?"

"No, but I know how to get there."

"Which direction, north, south, east, or west?" Jerry said facetiously.

"I'll have to tell you as we go along. I'm not familiar with names out here, just how to get there."

"You know, Joshua, you are a mystery. You know where you want to go, but don't have the slightest idea where it is. What a paradox! No one will ever believe this," Jerry said, scratching his head.

"Well, you know the way we started out yesterday," Joshua said. "We have to go in that same direction. As we go along, I'll know where to go from there."

"Amazing. I have to admit I have never had an experience like this in my life before. Sounds like the way we look for oil. You'd make a good geologist."

"Did you ever imagine such a thing, Martha Dell?" Jerry said to his wife, jokingly. "He doesn't know where he wants to go, but he knows how to get there."

"You're doing just fine, Jerry. Five more miles up the road and then turn right," Joshua directed him.

They all had fun at the bizarre way Joshua had of giving directions, never knowing where he was going, but knowing precisely each turn they had to take to get there.

The drive into the mountains turned out to be exciting. Though the snow had stopped falling, the road was slippery from the drifting snow and wet slush. The sun was shining, and the sky was soft powder blue, with no trace of pollution. The conversation in the car was light and jovial.

Finally, after innumerable turns in every which direction, they arrived at their destination. Jerry and Martha Dell were astounded that they'd found the place.

"This is it, turn right here, Jerry!"

"Are you sure this is it?"

"Yes, I'm certain."

"Are they expecting you?"

"No, but that's all right. They are nice people. They will welcome us."

"If you say so."

Driving up along the road to the registration office, Jerry dropped Joshua off at the entrance, then parked the car.

"Can I help you, sir?"

"Yes, my name is Joshua. I've heard good things about your community and I was hoping I might be allowed to attend some of your services."

"Do you have personal acquaintances in our community?"

"No."

"Let me call one of the elders to come and meet with you. Would you please take a seat in the waiting room across the hall? Someone will be with you in a moment."

"Thank you."

Jerry and Martha Dell walked into the lobby, and entered the small parlor where Joshua was sitting.

"This is a nice place. What is it?" Jerry asked Joshua.

"A retreat for evangelicals. The people are very gentle and caring, but they are anxious about the End Times, which they feel are imminent. Without proper guidance they can wander too far in dangerous paths and hurt themselves and their families."

"Why is it important for you to come way up here, especially since they don't even know you?" Martha Dell asked.

"Because I know they will listen and I will be able to help them."

"Joshua, I'll just sit back and continue to be bewildered. It's an experience just watching you. You're different, you know?" Jerry said good-naturedly.

"Really?" Joshua replied with a grin.

"Good morning," the man said as he entered. "I am John Beasley, an elder with our group here. How can I be of service to you?"

As he was speaking, Joshua and his two companions rose to greet him.

"My name is Joshua, and these are friends Jerry and Martha Dell Lewis, who were nice enough to drive me here to visit with you. I appreciate your kindness in meeting with us since we did not call beforehand. I admire the work you and your people are doing and I was hoping I could spend a little time here visiting with your family."

"Won't you all be seated?" the elder said as he sat down.

"It is very kind of you to say such nice things about us. We are quite proud of our work, and pray God will continue to bless us. Could you tell me why you would like to spend time with us?"

"Yes. I would like to learn more about your ways and what your vision might be for the future. I would also like, if it is not out of place, to spend some time talking with the elders and teachers in your community, to better understand your way of life."

"We don't often have people making requests like this, but I don't think it would be a problem. When would you like to come and spend time with us?"

"Perhaps tomorrow, and for the next few days, if that is acceptable."

"That would be all right. So, we can expect you tomorrow, before lunch or before supper?"

"Before lunch?"

"We will expect you tomorrow before lunch. I will tell the others, so they can also expect you."

"Thank you very much, Mr. Beasley," Joshua said as they all rose to take their leave.

"Good day," the elder said as he left the room.

"Joshua, you pulled it off," Jerry said as they were walking out the front door.

"I told you they are nice people."

"I'm sure he doesn't have the slightest idea of what you have up your sleeve."

"Well, you don't expect me to tell him everything. He would have immediately become wary and had reservations about me staying there. Remember, one must be 'simple as a dove, but sly as a fox.' "

"You follow that one to perfection, though more the 'sly as a fox' part."

Joshua smiled.

Leaving the retreat, they drove back down to the highway.

"We might as well stop off for lunch before we go back," Jerry suggested.

Everyone agreed.

That night was Joshua's last at the fellowship house. Though no one saw much of him in the few days he was there, his mere presence brought a peaceful feeling to the community, evidenced by the sadness each one felt when it was announced that he would be leaving the next day. The group decided to have a little going-away party for him that night, to show that they really appreciated his being with them. He was only a stranger passing through, but in a subtle way he touched each of them deeply, and in a way each would never forget.

The next day Jerry drove Joshua back to the retreat. The two had become close in the short time they spent together, and though Jerry was not ordinarily an emotional man, the tears in his eyes showed the sadness he felt at Joshua's departure.

"I'm going to miss you, young man. Have a good journey, and I know God always goes with you. My wife and I wanted you to have this little memento for your travels."

He gave Joshua a small package.

"Open it when you get inside. I don't like sentimental farewells."

With that he gave Joshua a hug. Joshua put his hand on his shoulder and blessed him, and they parted.

Two of the elders, an older man in his sixties, named John Moore, and another gentleman, named Horace Mansfield, met Joshua inside and welcomed him. They were proper, quite formal, but obviously good, sincere men. They immediately conducted Joshua on a tour of the facility, which consisted of several large apartment buildings, a spacious community room, and a large main building housing the offices and dining room, as well as a large auditorium that doubled as a church. It was all tastefully, though austerely, furnished, as is quite common among people of the Book. Joshua was impressed with the matter-of-fact, no-nonsense approach to their way of life. He noticed, however, that although he himself spoke the everyday language of the people, these people spoke more a language that was similar to Bible language of a past age.

"Joshua, this is our auditorium," one of the elders told him. "Although there are only three hundred of us living here, the auditorium has a capacity of six hundred, to accommodate larger crowds when we have a guest speaker or gospel concert. We will be having a concert tomorrow evening which we hope you will enjoy."

Exiting the building, they brought Joshua to a car waiting outside. As they entered the senior elder told the driver to drive them to the apartment building where Joshua would be staying. It was farther up on the mountainside, with a view across the valley.

"This will be your apartment during the time you will be with us," Mr. Mansfield said. "We hope the accommodations are adequate. We don't charge guests, but you might wish to leave a donation with us when you leave. Here is a key to your apartment. Now, make yourself at home, and we hope you enjoy your visit with us. We have lunch at twelve o'clock in the dining room. We will introduce you to the people when we meet there. Not everyone chooses to eat in the dining room, but there will be a good number there whom you can meet."

"Thank you very much, I am grateful for your kindness. I am sure I will enjoy my stay here."

When the men left, Joshua opened the gift that Jerry and Martha Dell gave him. It was an ancient Roman coin with Caesar's image engraved on one side. With the coin was a little note: "Thought this might bring back memories. Love,

Jerry and Martha Dell." Joshua laughed heartily. As he put the coin and note back in the box, he noticed two $100 bills folded and tucked into the bottom of the box.

Joshua stood looking out the window across the valley, at the magnificent view spread out before his eyes. "The heavens show forth the glory of God, and the firmament boasts of his handiwork."

Joshua sat in a chair before the large picture window and thought for the longest time, praying that future generations would preserve, untouched and unspoiled, his Father's masterpieces in creation, so children of the future would still be able to find God in their breathtaking majesty.

As he sat there deep in thought, his remarkable vision scanned the whole planet and the beautiful natural treasures his Father placed in creation for His children's inspiration and enjoyment. "My Father created this world with such love, how can people so ruthlessly destroy it just for money?" he thought. "There is an awesome intangible value in nature's pristine beauty. For some human beings it is their only contact with their Creator. There are others who can find God only in the magnificence of His creation and nowhere else. Unless people learn to value my Father's gifts of natural masterpieces, one by one they will be destroyed, and sold for money, until there is nothing left to remind the world of its Creator. God's masterpieces have such intrinsic, far-reaching value that no amount of material gain can ever justify their destruction."

It was soon time for lunch. As Joshua began walking down the road to the dining room, others met him along the way and introduced themselves.

"You're the new guest, I presume," said a man on his way to lunch with his family. "My name is Jon, and this my wife Klara, and my children, Clarissa, Joselda, and Pieter. Welcome to our community."

"Thank you, my name is Joshua. Your people are very gracious. Do you all live here?"

"Yes, we all originally came from other parts of the country. Our church was concerned about the approaching millennium, so the national committee decided to build this place in preparation for the End Times, for any who wanted to come and live here. So, yes, we *have* come from different parts of the country. We joined this community life so, in whatever time we have left, we can live as the early Christians did, for one another in love and peace."

"What is the name of your organization?"

"The Church of God in Christ. We are evangelical and follow the Bible strictly."

As people assembled for lunch, there was total silence in the dining room. When everyone was there, the senior elder, Matthias Stone, stood to pray the grace. "Father in Heaven, thou has generously given us this daily bread today. We are grateful to thee for thy beneficence toward us. Some of us are suffering from Satan's evil, and are sick in bed. Raise them up, Lord, to come back and continue their service to the community. Bless our guest, Brother Joshua, who just came among us to learn about our way of life. Be gracious to him and grant him a peaceful and fruitful stay here. And bless this food, Lord, to renew our strength to continue thy work. We ask this in the name of Jesus the Lord."

To which everyone added a loud "Amen."

The room was still silent. A man approached a lectern and began to read from the scriptures. "Today our reading is from the Book of Revelation, Chapter fourteen, verses fourteen to twenty.

" 'And I looked, and behold, a white cloud, and upon the cloud *one* sat like unto the Son of man, having on his head a golden crown, and in his hand a sharp sickle. And another angel came out of the temple, crying with a loud voice to him that sat on the cloud, "Thrust in thy sickle, and reap: for the time is come for thee to reap; for the harvest of the earth is ripe." And he that sat on the cloud thrust in his sickle on the earth; and the earth was reaped.

" 'And another angel came out of the temple which is in heaven, he also having a sharp sickle. And another angel came out from the altar, which had power over fire; and cried with a loud cry to him that had the sharp sickle, saying, "Thrust in thy sharp sickle, and gather the clusters of the vine of the earth; for her grapes are fully ripe." And the angel thrust in his sickle into the earth, and gathered the vine of the earth, and cast *it* into the great winepress of the wrath of God. And the winepress was trodden without the city, and blood came out of the winepress, even unto the horse bridles, by the space of a thousand *and* six hundred furlongs.' "

When the reading was finished, the people were expected to meditate on its meaning, so they still ate in silence.

After lunch, the people left the dining room and went back to their assigned jobs. Not everyone worked at the retreat. Many had jobs in Denver or other places nearby. The only ones present for the lunch were people employed by the center. As they filed out of the dining hall, an elder approached Joshua and struck up a conversation with him.

"Brother Joshua, welcome to our family. My name is Edward James. Did you enjoy your lunch?"

"Very much," Joshua replied.

"How about the quiet meal and the reading?"

"An interesting practice. In the old monastic tradition," he responded.

"Yes, I have been told the monks still read scripture while eating their meals. Did you enjoy the reading?"

"Well, I would not call it entertaining. Do your people think that reading is a prophecy still to be fulfilled?"

"Of course. In fact, the time may be fast approaching, our scripture experts tell us."

Joshua listened politely, but said nothing.

"Do you read the Bible, Brother Joshua?"

"In its fulfillment," Joshua replied.

"Now, that's an answer I haven't heard before. I will have to think on that one. Quite an answer, quite an answer, young man. I hope you have a pleasant stay with us. Know that you are most welcome here, so feel at home and enjoy your visit and the beautiful scenery as well."

"Thank you, Edward."

The man took a side path. Joshua wandered off into the woods, along a path to the top of the mountain, with its vast panorama of fields and hills spread out before him, reminding him of the high mountain of long ago where he was shown all the kingdoms of the earth. He could still see all the kingdoms of the earth. He did not need to be on a high mountain. The whole of creation in all its detail was forever present to him.

As he looked across the hills and valleys, sadness overwhelmed him. An ominous vision flashed across his mind and clouded the happy time he had just experienced with these simple and honest people. "Father, I tried to reach out to those people in the cult, but they would not listen. They tried to do me harm, and I forgave them. In their sick delusions they thought they were doing good. So many people do terrible things to others, convinced that what they are doing is justified because they are protecting some righteous cause.

"Father, now that they are no more, pity them and in your limitless mercy pardon them for the evil they have done and do not be harsh to them, for what they had done they thought was right. It pains me to see people destroyed like that, so needlessly, and for no purpose. Comfort their families and loved ones left behind. Grant them some measure of understanding to ease their pain."

Finished praying, he turned and walked down the mountain to his apartment and rested. It was a full two hours before he was awakened by a phone call.

"Hello, Joshua speaking."

"Joshua, I hope I am not disturbing you."

"Not at all."

"Joshua, this is John Beasley. If you are not occupied, would you care to visit with a few of the elders and myself? They would very much like to make your acquaintance."

"I would be happy to. Where shall I meet you?"

"Down at the center. I will meet you in the lobby."

"I'll be there in a few minutes."

The elders were all fine men, chosen by the community for their integrity and also for their wisdom. They had a reputation for being compassionate men. In apparent obedience to St. Paul's injunction, there were no women elders. Everyone seemed to agree that that was what St. Paul meant, so there was little conflict in the church over the matter.

As Joshua walked down toward the center, he noticed that, although it was only four in the afternoon, the sky was unusually dark and the snow was falling heavily. The atmosphere seemed to mirror an ominous foreboding of things happening and about to happen. Walking in the snow was a pleasant distraction that momentarily lifted his spirits. He liked walking in the snow. It was clean and pure and fresh, and exhilarating.

"Thank you for coming down, Joshua," Mr. Beasley said.

"I was looking forward to meeting your colleagues."

"Let me bring you into the office, where it is more private."

The office was a small conference room where the elders met on informal occasions. As Joshua and Mr. Beasley entered, the other elders stood in welcome. There were five in all, older men, and quite dignified. After the customary introductions, one of the elders immediately stood out, a Mr. Charles Pomeroy. He was quite round, with a jolly expression that seemed to be a permanent feature of his personality. It was difficult not to smile when looking at him, especially when he was speaking, as his dark eyes opened wide, his eyebrows constantly arched, and his lips pursed, as if he had just tasted a raw lemon. His ready humor matched his facial expressions, giving everyone who met him the impression he was just born that way.

"Please take a seat for yourself, Mr. Joshua, Joshua, or whatever it is that people call you," said Mr. Pomeroy. "Do you have a first name or a surname or whichever it is that is missing?"

"No, that's my only name," Joshua responded.

"Quite unusual, as I expect you yourself are, sir. Of course, I mean that in the most complimentary way."

"People tell me I am not the usual stranger walking down the street, but then, isn't each one special and unique? I can see, Mr. Pomeroy, God was indeed in a generous good mood when he fashioned you also. Your happy spirit and ready wit testify to that."

Everyone laughed at how readily their guest had quipped with their witty colleague.

"Touché, Mr. Joshua, touché! You have a fine mind as well as a ready wit yourself. I think I like you already."

Matthias Stone broke into the conversation and addressed Joshua. "Joshua, I hope you feel at home among us. We are happy to have you spend some time here. Those who have already met you are quite impressed. I and my colleagues thought it might be nice to invite you to spend some time with us, so you can get to know us and we can learn more about you. Might I ask where you live?"

"My home is not hence. I come from an entirely different world, which is quite far from here and yet not far at all."

"May I ask where you were born?"

"I was born in Bethlehem."

"In which state, there are quite a few Bethlehems?"

"In Judea."

"You are Jewish then."

"Yes."

"I hope you feel comfortable among this large extended Christian family of ours."

"Perfectly at home, Mr. Stone."

"Are you familiar with Christian teachings?"

"Yes, quite familiar, though I find that many Christians are not. I have found very few who really know Jesus in any depth, which is sad, because he really is the Christian religion, not theology or the Bible."

"That is a remarkable observation, Joshua," another elder, Edward James, commented. He was the one who had met Joshua earlier outside the dining room. "How do you mean that the Bible is not the Christian religion. Do you not look upon the Bible as the sole rule of the Christian faith?"

"No, Jesus is the rule of the Christian faith."

"But do we not get to know Jesus and his teachings through study of the Bible?"

"That is one way, but Jesus never told anyone to write a Bible. The early Christian teachers wrote the New Testament part of the Bible, so it shares only as much authority as the early Church had to write it. Jesus gave authority to the apostles and to those upon whom the apostles would lay their hands in imparting their authority. Jesus committed his message to them; they are and will always be the rule of faith in Jesus' mind. The New Testament is an expression of a part of their teaching. In keeping with his promise to send the Holy Spirit, Jesus has been guiding the apostles through the centuries in an ever-deepening understanding of his message. To go back to the book alone is to deny the Holy Spirit's two thousand years of guidance, and all the growth in understanding that has taken place in those two thousand years."

The men were shocked that this wanderer should have such a profound understanding of the essence of the Christian religion. But they were not a little taken aback by his comment that Jesus never gave anyone a book, as the foundation of *their* religion was the Bible. For them the Bible alone contained all that one must know about Jesus' teachings and one's personal salvation.

They were, however, not offended as much as surprised. Joshua was not the slightest bit offensive or argumentative in what he said. He was merely responding to their questions in a calm objective statement.

"Joshua," Mr. Beasley said, "you surprise us with your understanding of Jesus' teachings. You have an uncanny grasp of the mind of Jesus for a Jew."

"Maybe because I am a Jew."

"Well taken, young man. It is a joy talking with you. It is a blessing that you have come to spend time with us," one of the other elders commented. "But when Church leaders of the past have led such scandalous lives, don't you think people were justified in going off on their own, out of loyalty to Jesus?"

"Would Paul have been loyal to Jesus if, because he disagreed with Peter on important matters, he went off and started his own religion, saying, 'I alone am worthy to spread the gospel because Peter is a hypocrite?' Or would Barnabas have been loyal to Jesus if he started his own religion because he couldn't get along with Paul? Jesus never guaranteed personal sanctity to the leaders of his community, only that he would guarantee the faithful transmission of his gospel until the end of time."

"For a man who has never been trained in these matters you have given us much to think about. We are pleased that you took time to sit and talk with us today. We would like to mull over the matters we just discussed, and perhaps, we could meet again tomorrow?"

"That would be fine. You have great humility and sincerity, gentlemen, to take so seriously the observations of a stranger concerning matters that affect you so deeply. I know you wish to follow Jesus with honesty and purity of heart."

When Joshua left, the elders became engrossed in an intense discussion as to the place of the Bible in Christianity. What the stranger said made a lot of sense, but to accept that premise would mean they would have to alter their thinking of a lifetime, everything they had been taught from childhood.

"My brothers," Mr. Pomeroy said, "what the stranger spoke about has crossed my mind many times, but I did not have the courage to even think about. Now that he has brought it to our attention so vividly, we are forced to consider it. The Book did not just drop down out of heaven. Who said we have to accept it for our salvation? People cannot just decide that and then impose it on the whole world. Only someone with authority could say that the Book is authentic and that we must accept it. Even St. Augustine said that he accepted the Bible as the inspired word of God because the Church said so, otherwise he would have no obligation to accept it as inspired any more than any other religious book. So, maybe, as much as it tears at my heart, we must reconsider the basic premises of our faith."

"Wait a minute, Charles!" interrupted Matthias Stone, "let's not be too quick to question something so sacred as the very foundations of our faith. We have been taught since childhood that the Bible is the sole rule of faith. There is a validity to that statement that should never be questioned."

"But, my dear Matthias," Charles responded, "attachment to a premise has to have reason behind it. What is the basis for accepting the Bible as the sole rule of faith? Peter said in his holy epistle that we must have a reason for our faith. What is the reason we believe that the Bible is the sole rule of faith? Because Martin Luther said so? What reason did he have, other than that he had become disillusioned with authority. And in rejecting that authority, he had no other recourse but to put his total faith in the Book, a book which Jesus never told anyone to write, a book which has authority only because the Church wrote it. So, even the Book's authority comes from the Church."

"Charles," Edward James interrupted, "why do you have to upset things? We have lived with this all our lives, why change now?"

"Edward, I am not upsetting anyone. I am merely responding to an issue that was raised by a total stranger who happens to be a Jew. Even he questions the premise of our faith, though he is not one of us."

"Gentlemen, gentlemen," John interjected, "let us try to be calm. I know it is going to be a troubling issue, and all the more reason why we have to approach it calmly, and even more important, with respect for each other's understandable concerns. If I may, I see the issue a little differently. I can understand and accept that Jesus gave authority to the apostles and something special, whatever that was, to Peter, whom he expected to guide the others when his own faith was confirmed. As they chose others and laid their hands on them, choosing them to succeed them, their authority passed on to their successors. I can understand and accept that. But my conviction is that as time went on their successors become corrupt, thus betraying their commitment to Christ. Christians then took things into their own hands and adopted the Bible as their guide in matters of faith. This we have inherited to this day."

"Now, John," Charles continued, "my question is this, and I did not pick this up from the stranger. This has been troubling me for a long time, but I dared not express it. When Christian people became disillusioned with the Church authorities because of their personal corruption, did they have the right to take that authority on themselves? Who gave them the authority to do that? No one has ever shown that the Church leaders officially taught anything contradictory to Jesus' teachings, in spite of their scandalous personal lives. In fact they remained remarkably faithful to the teachings of Jesus."

"That is debatable, Charles," Edward remarked. "Some of them approved things that were downright criminal."

"What they did or approved is different from teaching

something officially. We have all done things that are abominable, but our churches didn't teach those things. I feel the bottom line is that Jesus gave us an official community and guaranteed to be with that community and its leaders, though he did not guarantee the holiness of its leaders. Our forefathers rejected that community and the authority of its leaders. So, now we have a book, but no authority to teach."

"I don't agree," John replied. "The elders in each denomination have taken on that authority."

"Precisely, they have taken on that authority. But my question is, 'Who gave them the right to do that?' They couldn't just say, 'Well, Jesus, I'm taking over now, so you'll have to deal with me. You'll have to work through me.' That's downright presumptuous. I don't feel *I* have the authority to go off and start a religion. Do *you?*"

"Charles, you make a powerful statement of your position," Edward commented. "I can understand your viewpoint and I admit it makes sense, but I can't believe that I have been following a delusion all my life. I feel I have to be faithful to what I was taught from my childhood. It is to me a sacred heritage."

"Gentlemen, the discussion has been a fruitful one," John said, by way of wrapping up the meeting. "I suggest we study the matter and pray very hard over it. Perhaps, when our friend comes to meet with us tomorrow we can have some of these issues resolved. Thank you all for being considerate of one another. See you all at supper."

CHAPTER 11

THE READING AT supper was from the Second Letter of
Peter, Chapter 3, verses 8 to 18. " 'But, beloved, be not ig-
norant of this one thing, that one day is with the Lord as a
thousand years, and a thousand years as one day. The Lord
is not slack concerning his promise, as some men count
slackness; but is longsuffering to us-ward, not willing that
any should perish, but that all should come to repentance.
But the day of the Lord will come as a thief in the night; in
the which the heavens shall pass away with a great noise,
and the elements shall melt with fervent heat, the earth also
and the works that are therein shall be burned up. Seeing
then that all these things shall be dissolved, what manner of
persons ought ye to be in all holy conversation and godli-
ness, looking for and hasting unto the coming of the day of
God, wherein the heavens being on fire shall be dissolved,

and the elements shall melt with fervent heat? Nevertheless we, according to his promise, look for new heavens and a new earth, wherein dwelleth righteousness.

" 'Wherefore, beloved, seeing that ye look for such things, be diligent that ye may be found of him in peace, without spot, and blameless. And account that the long-suffering of our Lord is salvation; even as our beloved brother Paul also according to the wisdom given unto him hath written unto you; As also in all his epistles, speaking in them of these things; in which are some things hard to be understood, which they that are unlearned and unstable wrest, as they do also the other scriptures, unto their own destruction.

" 'Ye therefore, beloved, seeing ye know these things before, beware lest ye also, being led away with the error of the wicked, fall from your own steadfastness. But grow in grace, and in the knowledge of our Lord and Savior Jesus Christ. To him be glory both now and for ever. Amen.' "

After supper many gathered in the large community center, which consisted of one large room broken into quiet areas where people conversed or played games. There were smaller rooms off the main room where people watched television, or have quiet time with friends.

The recreation was interrupted by a special news announcement. "An evangelical community in upstate New York, which had been the subject of concern to local officials, had just within the last hour, fallen victim to a bizarre tragedy. All hundred and five members of the community were found dead by a local hunter. They had apparently taken their own lives. This was the final episode in their quest for deliverance from what they frequently referred to as this 'wicked and adulterous age.'

"Their Leader, the Reverend Miller, was among the victims. In his hand was a letter, just recently released to the news. It stated that he and his followers had taken this step as a way of disassociating themselves from the evil of this present age and purifying themselves for the Lord, so they would be worthy to enter into the kingdom innocent and unsullied by the evil surrounding them. In this way they could be worthy to follow the Lamb in spotless white robes.

"The local clergy stated in an interview that they had tried on numerous occasions to meet with the leaders of the group. However, their overtures were rejected. Others tried to talk with them, but to no avail. The clergy as well as the local townsfolk were deeply shaken over the terrible incident."

Joshua could not bear to listen to the news announcement. He had known it already and the thought had been weighing on his heart all afternoon. He walked up to his apartment and prayed for the hapless victims, as he stared out at the flickering lights sprinkled throughout the valley. The melancholy winter scene soothed his troubled spirit.

The next day's meeting with the elders opened with a prayer. Everyone, even Joshua, had a heavy heart, still troubled over the news from the night before.

"Joshua," John said, by way of opener, "you occasioned quite a discussion after yesterday's meeting. We discussed at length the issues you raised at the meeting, and we are curious as to why you said the things you did. You gave the impression that you are searching. Perhaps you are interested in Christianity?"

Joshua smiled. "I have been interested in Christianity longer than any of you could imagine. My raising of those issues yesterday was in response to your questions, not an expression, however, of my own searching. I feel they are important issues, which the Christian communities throughout the world must address, if they want to truly follow all that Jesus taught. The sad news last night dramatizes the dangers of a community that lacks true guidance, where a person assumes authority on his own and leads the community into great peril."

"Yes, we are all deeply saddened over that horrible tragedy. It occasioned much soul-searching," Edward said. "However, even though we are concerned about the end of the world, we are really not in the same situation as that unfortunate community. We do have an authentic authority. Elders are chosen by the community, and receive their call from the community. The community gives us the authority to teach and to govern."

"Quite a democratic process!" Joshua responded. "Is that the way Jesus established the Church, and the way the apostles passed on their authority?"

"Not exactly," John replied.

"Well, that should be the key to understanding the instructions Jesus gave to the apostles for the passing on of authority, if you want to be faithful to Jesus," Joshua responded. "It is essential to follow what Jesus established through the apostles, otherwise any group can presume to give authority to someone. But why should God be expected to honor what they have decided? That is a serious problem in Christianity, people making their own plans and expecting God to do what they decide. God does not work that way. People are expected to do things the way He has directed, then they have the assurance of God's blessing and guidance."

"Joshua, you don't make it easy for us. For all these many years, we have lived this way and now you shake our faith, and suggest that what we have been doing is wrong."

"Your personal lives are still holy. You are good people and God blesses your sincerity, and your honesty. So, you need not fear that your lives have not been pleasing to God."

"Joshua," Charles interjected, "you speak with such authority and with such good sense that we feel we should hear you out. This is not easy for us, but our small congregation has always tried to be open to wherever God leads us. Even though you are a stranger in our midst, we listen with humility and weigh in a prayerful manner what you share with us. Are we now to find a church where these traditions are honored, do you think?"

"God is a gentle God. All He expects is your openness to His grace. In time He will lead you to where He wants you to be. In the meantime, just live out each day prayerfully. You need not be anxious."

"Joshua, we have come here as an End Time community because we thought that, following the signs in the scriptures, the end of the world was imminent. What do you think?" Charles asked him.

"Charles, why would anyone think that this particular year is more significant than any other year?"

"Because it is the beginning of the new millennium," Charles answered, "and the thousandth year is fraught with much scriptural meaning. Also there are so many signs which scripture had pointed out as preceding the End Times."

"If you are referring to the two thousandth anniversary of Jesus' birth, that is long past. Jesus was born in 4 B.C. A monk miscalculated the time of Jesus' birth so the new millennium began four years ago. Besides, you don't think that God makes decisions based on human calendars, do you? The world will not end until my Father's entire plan is accomplished. That is not calculated according to people's calendar. His creation is still in the process of an evolving perfection, as all things are gathered into His Son. When all things are made perfect in His Son, then the work of creation is accomplished, and not before. So, do not be afraid. There is no need to isolate yourselves like this. Your work as his followers is to be a light to the dark world around you, so others can learn to recognize the beauty of God's Son in each of you, his disciples. That you cannot do when you cut yourselves off from the world. Your goodness must witness to his enduring presence in the world, so others may be drawn to him."

"What a beautiful way for God to work. It is so simple, yet makes so much sense. Why would God want His creation to come to an end when it is still so far from perfection," John Beasley commented. He then continued, "Joshua, how do you view the kingdom of God?"

"The kingdom of God is like a King who entrusted a vast and priceless treasure to his servants. He gave them full responsibility for dispensing that treasure to those in his kingdom and to draw into the kingdom all other people living in the land. Some of the servants were good people, some were bad, but they still were responsible. Others came along who did not like the King's servants, and convinced some of the people that they now possessed the treasure, and that the people should follow them, though the King had never given them such authority. For many years, the kingdom split into endless factions hostile to the King's servants and their disciples. As time went on, these groups began to wither and fade away because they did not have a lasting treasure, and the people suffered want.

"Then came a humble and righteous leader of the King's servants. He truly loved the King and not just the kingdom. His kindness and humility caused those who had broken away to look into their hearts, and consider what would truly please the King. It was then that all the wandering groups gathered together in the kingdom and worked together to further the King's wishes. Indeed, the whole world was then blessed because all the factions in the kingdom worked together to make known the King's name. The kingdom soon encompassed the earth, and from that time on there was truly a thousand years of Messianic prosperity as all peoples and all things were gathered together in the Son's name."

"How beautiful, Joshua, how beautiful!" Charles said, teary-eyed. "Joshua, who are you really? You do not speak like a wandering stranger. You do not speak like a Jew who had never followed Jesus. You do not even speak like a clergyman. No clergyman ever spoke the way you speak, and with such authority, as if you knew what others do not know. Whoever you are, thank you, thank you for what you have given to us. We have much to think about, and many decisions to make."

The others quite agreed, and as there was little more that could be said, they rose and hugged their guest, asking him if he could meet with them again to discuss other matters. He agreed. With that the meeting adjourned.

Joshua's thoughts for the rest of the day were many. Things were happening in various parts of the world. There were tornadoes and earthquakes, wars and insurrections, floods and drought. Joshua felt the pain of all the suffering these calamities caused, and he spent quiet time as he walked among the people and in the forests praying to his Father to ease the pain of the victims, and bring speedily home those who had died. He knew his Father always listened and answered his prayers, but not in ways that were clear to others.

He also prayed for the good people living in this little community. They were kindly, sincere people who wanted to live in a way that would be pleasing to God. Joshua felt close to them and asked his Father's special blessing upon them.

Word about Joshua spread fast through the group. At first he seemed like a quiet, private man, easy to talk to when someone approached him, but one who guarded his privacy. Everyone knew he was a guest and he was treated as one, graciously and with consideration. Little children seemed to be drawn to him, and when they found him alone, were not at all reluctant to engage him in child talk, which he seemed to enjoy immensely. One day he made a snowball, and threw it to one of the boys. When the boy caught it, to his surprise, it was not a snowball, but a beautifully colored rubber ball, warm to the touch, without losing its warmth from being in the snow.

"How did you do that, mister?" a young boy asked.

Joshua just smiled and continued playing with the children.

A little girl approached him on one occasion, and told Joshua her brother was very sick, and her mother and father were worried about him. She was afraid he might die. "Would you pray for him, Joshua, because you are a good man, and God will listen to your prayers," she said.

"I will pray for him. Do not worry your little head about him. Your brother will be all right."

"But could you please come to the house and see him, and pray over him?"

Joshua followed as the girl took him by the hand and led him to her home. When they reached the house, the girl walked in bringing Joshua with her. Her mother was shocked.

"Mommy, I brought my friend Joshua to visit Tommy, and pray over him."

"I am so sorry, sir, if my daughter inconvenienced you in any way. She is sometimes so forward."

"I would be happy to pray over your son."

"He is so terribly ill," the mother told Joshua. "The doctor said there is little that can be done for him. Bringing him to the hospital would not be of much use, as his sickness is terminal. We have prayed so hard for him. I did not want to pray for God to keep him here, if God really wants him home, but in my heart, I want more than anything for him to get better, even if there is no hope."

"There is always hope. Do not be anxious, my Father has answered your prayers and the prayers of little Jacqueline here. Where is your son?"

"In the bedroom."

"May I see him?"

"Yes, but he may be resting."

As the three entered the room, the boy feebly turned his head and looked over at them, as Joshua walked toward the bed. Reaching out, he placed his hand on the boy's head, and prayed: "Father, bless this little boy who has already suffered much. Heal him, bring him back to health, and restore him to his family."

Then, taking the boy by the hand, he told the boy to sit up. When he did, a smile crossed his face, and he cried out, "Mommy, Mommy, I am better. I feel so good, Mommy. Can I have something to eat, I am so hungry."

Seeing her brother was better, Jacqueline jumped up and down, screaming out loud, "Tommy's better, Tommy's better. I knew Joshua would make him better. Thank you, Joshua. Thank you."

The mother put her arms around her son and cried tears of joy and gratitude.

"Thank you, oh, thank you so much, Joshua! My daughter was right. She told me I should ask you to pray for our son. She said you were a good man and that God would certainly listen to your prayers. She was right. Little children can recognize goodness even in a stranger. You *are* a good man, and God *does* listen to you."

"It is your faith and your child's faith that have done this. Even though my Father was going to bring Tommy home, your resignation to my Father's will touched His heart, so He gave Tommy back to you and your family."

It did not take long before the news spread, and the more it spread the more the story changed. When word of it reached the elders, they were deeply moved. At first they were surprised, but as they thought about it, they began to wonder all the more about this unusual man who had just wandered into their midst. They went to the family's house to see if the rumor was really true. And when they realized that there was no possible explanation other than that God had truly answered their prayers, they left with much to think about.

After Tommy's healing, Joshua tried to withdraw up into the woods, but someone had seen him. Soon, others came to him with those who were sick and troubled. Always compassionate and unable to resist the pleas of the helpless, Joshua comforted the troubled and healed the sick and those with crippled limbs.

The next day he met again with the elders. This time they treated him with almost a reverence. Joshua noticed it and it made him uncomfortable. "Why are you so different today? Yesterday we could talk and enjoy a conversation. Today you act differently. Be the way you were yesterday, so we can enjoy ourselves!"

They laughed, and were soon back to normal.

"Joshua, that was nice what you did for that family with the sick child," Edward said.

"What did I do?" Joshua asked by way of finding out what they knew.

"You prayed over him and God answered your prayer," Edward responded.

Satisfied that they intended to respect his privacy, Joshua remarked, "Yes, God is always by our side when we need Him."

"We appreciate your spending time with us, Joshua," John said. "We have been discussing among ourselves what we talked about yesterday. Charles reminded us of Jesus' prayer at the Last Supper, when he was so concerned about unity. It is a remarkable prayer because, at the time, the apostles were one. It was almost as if Jesus could see what would eventually happen and prayed that wound would be healed and his family would again become one. After much discussion, we decided to talk to our people and share with them our thoughts on this matter. We decided to ask if they would consider responding to that prayer of Jesus' and work with us as we meet with others to plan for real unity. There is an ecumenical spirit afloat but it does not go very deep. It is more a token gesture toward unity, but without any real intention to become one. What we would like to do is take concrete steps to meet with others and take serious steps toward unity with those churches whose roots go deepest into history. In this way we will be responding in a genuine way to Jesus' concern for unity in his family."

"It took great courage and humility for you to agree to

such a decision. You can be sure God will richly reward you for your faithfulness," Joshua replied.

"We discussed other options also, like merging with another church, but we are not yet ready for that. Maybe somewhere along the line, when we feel more comfortable with this new way of thinking, we could consider a move as dramatic as that. At this point, however, we must respect our people's feelings and their long-standing resistance to other churches. Maybe in time, when we have grown a bit more spiritually, we could consider a move like that, but at this point it would be too much of a shock to everyone."

"But you make us think, Joshua, and for that we are grateful. Will you be staying with us for a while longer?" Matthias commented. It was difficult for Matthias to go along with the others. He was attached to the old ways, and did not make changes easily, especially radical ones such as his group was considering. But being a thoughtful and dispassionate man, he would work hard at trying to understand what the others grasped so easily.

"Today will be my last day," Joshua said. "It has been a most enjoyable stay among you and your people. Your community is remarkable in its dedication to the real substance of Jesus' spirit. You will be a light and a source of strength to many others as they follow you in the journey you are about to undertake."

"Thank you, Joshua. We will never forget you. You will be forever in our prayers," John said, as his voice began to choke up.

Having shared with Joshua the results of their long private meetings, and the courageous decision, there was little more to talk about, Charles, the entertainer in the group, suggested they have a little private party and invite some of their close friends in the community, as a farewell to their newfound friend. "It just happens that I have a rather good supply of beverages at my place. Perhaps we could meet there, say, at seven. That will give us a chance to spend some time with people in the dining room, then come back up to my place for the party."

To which everyone heartily agreed. Great idea!

At the end of the meeting, a crowd of grateful people was waiting outside for Joshua. They were men and women, and children as well. They were people who were healed, or grateful family members of persons healed. They had been told Joshua would take nothing for what he had done, so they came to express what he could not deny them, their heartfelt gratitude for restoring loved ones to health, and to their families. They promised they would never forget him as long as they lived and would show the same compassion to others as he had shown to them. It was a very touching expression of appreciation, shown in a way that was so simple, yet filled with meaning and sincerity. Joshua was moved to tears. No one had ever thanked him quite like this before. Yes, this was truly a family of caring disciples of Jesus. Though he appeared a simple wandering stranger who came into their midst with nothing, in their simplicity, they could see goodness and holiness beneath the trappings of poverty.

"You need not thank me. What I did I did because I love you, and I was moved by the pain I saw in your hearts. Now I am touched by your simple expression of gratitude. May my Father bless you and all your loved ones! I also bless you. Be assured I will think of you always."

As Joshua walked through the crowd, each one wanted to touch him. They felt he was someone sacred. Perhaps his goodness would rub off on them. They were much like the people of long ago, the same searching for meaning to their lives, the same painful emptiness and loneliness, the same fears and anxiety over children and loved ones. Being human is so painful, in spite of occasional fleeting joys. He could understand their frailty, and their fears. There was no pain that passed his vision unnoticed, no suffering about which he was not concerned. What a remarkable God!

At suppertime, everyone came to the dining room knowing that he would be there. A few hours ago, he was a homeless stranger. Few paid much attention to him. Now everyone wanted to see him and understand what made him so different and so special. He was gracious as they swarmed around him. To the children he paid special attention. He did not want them to ever forget him, and his kindness toward them. The tender memory buried in their hearts would one day be their strength, and for some, their salvation in troubled times.

He sat with a family that usually ate alone. They were a father, mother, and four children. None of them spoke. They could not hear nor could they speak. As kind as the community was, they did not know how to approach them or socialize with them. The family could not but feel their isolation, and knew it would always be this way. Two other people sat at the table with them. They were blind. The people who could not speak had befriended them and were their constant companions. As Joshua approached their table and sensed their sorry situation, tears filled his eyes.

"My name is Joshua," he said. The deaf people had seen him, but had not heard of his recent exploits. The blind persons heard people talking about him but could not understand what it was all about. When Joshua's voice reached the ears of the deaf ones, they heard sound for the first time. Joshua signaled for them to be calm and not make a scene. When Joshua looked at the blind persons, their eyes immediately met his and they saw light for the first time. They were startled and almost leapt for joy, but he signaled them also not to make a fuss, but just to act normal. They tried but could not restrain their joy. For the first time laughter and joy burst forth from their table. Those nearby wondered what was happening there, but never imagined what really took place. It was only afterward that the community found out the truth. Then their awe was without bounds.

Joshua stayed at the table for a few minutes, broke bread with the little group, then excused himself to attend the party at Charles' house. As he left the table, the others stood, walked over to him, and hugging him tightly, thanked him. He smiled at them, and bid them good night.

Fifteen or so people attended the party at Charles' house. It was a happy affair. Though some of the elders did not take alcoholic beverages, Charles and others of the guests did. Joshua accepted a glass of red wine, which he drank while nibbling on hors d'oeuvres. Everyone at the party was casually dressed, so Joshua could feel at home in his simple clothes. Had he dressed elegantly he would have indeed looked impressive. His lean, strong build, his handsome, finely cut features gave no hint of race or nationality, but faintly reflected qualities of each; the soft, slightly wavy hair, not closely cropped, his long, graceful fingers; his facile conversational skills and ready humor. All these features presented a stunning image of class.

When Charles spotted Joshua, he came over and welcomed him warmly. "You may have been here at our retreat for only a few hours, but you sure did turn us all upside down. Your lighthearted happy spirit has had its effect on all of us, Joshua. You have given spirituality and holiness a new and healthy definition which none of us will forget. After you leave, the memory of your goodness will be with us a long time. We will not forget you. Were we not afraid of blaspheming, what you have done here the past few days is so reminiscent of what took place in the gospels, we would have concluded that he had come to honor us with a visit."

Joshua's whimsical smile spoke volumes, but he said nothing. The message in the smile was not lost on the perceptive elder.

Each guest in turn approached Joshua and expressed appreciation for what he had given to their community, especially for his priceless direction for the future. At the end of the evening, Joshua spent a few minutes with Charles and John. They were the real movers in the community. They asked Joshua's prayers that God would grant them the courage to lead their people in the direction they knew Jesus wanted them to go. Joshua assured them that this was important to God and that they could count on His grace.

"Now, Joshua, how about yourself? What will you do now? Can we drive you somewhere?" John asked.

"I appreciate your offer, but I will be long gone by morning."

"Where will you go?" John continued.

"Farther out west. There will be difficult times ahead, and people will need help."

"Can you share your concerns?" Charles asked.

"Certain ones, yes. The Church will be without a shepherd in a short time. For a brief period there will be terrible conflict in the Church, but then a new shepherd will emerge, a kindly, humble man who will be, not just in name, but in his heart a 'Servant of the servants of God.' He will love God's people more than the 'traditions of the ancients,' and will heal many wounds. By his humility he will draw people closer to the one fold and one shepherd Jesus dreamed of. Like David, he will be a man after the heart of God.

"There will also be natural disasters terrorizing many, as a calamity long predicted will come to pass. But it is not the end and people should not presume it to be so. It has been long in coming. People should have long ago heeded the warning of scientists, but they did not.

"But do not let these things frighten you; the end is nowhere near."

Though they asked Joshua further questions, he politely talked about other things. It was near midnight when the group dispersed.

The next morning Joshua was nowhere to be found, but his presence would be felt by those gentle people for much longer than the few days he walked among them.

CHAPTER 1 2

IT WAS THE weekend of the Jazz Festival. People came from all over the country for the experience, where the most popular musicians and some of the best chefs in the country plied their skills. Walking along the boardwalk was a balding young man in his fifties whose pixie-like features would bring a smile to the sourest-looking face. André was his name. He had come from the bayou just the day before to enjoy the festival.

"Hello, young man, you look mystified at all that's going on. Where are you from?" André said to the stranger who was soaking up the sights and sounds surrounding him.

"Just came to town to share in the excitement and watch the people enjoying the fun of being alive," the stranger responded without taking his eyes off the strange sights.

"First time in New Orleans?"

"Yes."

"It's a place all its own. The people are a happy people. We don't have the best reputation, but we're a happy, fun-loving people."

By this time, the two men were walking together.

"See that trolley car there?" André said.

"Yes."

"Well, I got to tell you a story about a trolley car. When I was a kid, a friend of mine and I had been out on the town. We had a little too much to drink, and had to get home. We couldn't find our car, but we knew the trolley line went right near our neighborhood at the end of the line. The conductor had left his trolley unattended, with the motor running, so we looked at each other, and then ran to the trolley, released the brake, and started driving down the track toward home. We almost made it when the cops caught up with us and parked their car on the tracks in front of the trolley. Well, what happened after that wasn't very funny, but the fun racing down the main street, with the bell ringing at one o'clock in the morning, was well worth it. My friend and I must have told that story a thousand times. It is as fresh in my memory today as the night it happened."

"I imagine this would be the only place in the country where people would see the humor in such a prank," Joshua commented.

"Life is hard down here, so we can't afford to take things too seriously. We rarely make a crisis out of anything if we can avoid it. Life is too short. So, whatever little plea-sures the Good Lord sends our way, we enjoy them, and we overlook a lot that other people would get all upset over."

Joshua smiled at André's earthy philosophy.

For the next two days André showed Joshua all the things that tourists never even hear of, and cafés and music not on any of the schedules. It was a poor people's version of the New Orleans Jazz Festival. One artist that André wanted Joshua to hear was Wynton Marsalis. A friend arranged for the two of them to attend his concert free. Both were totally absorbed in the remarkable trumpet playing of this extraordinary artist. The power and conviction of his music moved Joshua deeply. It was not religious music, but for Joshua religious expression was the natural goodness flowing from one's soul and lifting others to a greater awareness of God's presence in life. He saw that in Wynton's playing.

"His whole family are good people, Joshua. They're from right around here. I think you'd like them," André said as they were walking out.

"While we're here in the city, I'd like you to meet a friend. He's a real Cajun, his name is Earl, Earl Gervais, a little crazy like the rest of us, a nice kind of crazy, more high-spirited than crazy, I guess I should say. Well, I know you'd like him. He teaches high school, gets in trouble because he's always pushing Jesus to his students, not in a bad way, but in a way that makes some people squirm. He has a real live friendship with Jesus, and tries to share that with the kids. Some want him to just stick to the books. The Jesuit school where he taught kicked him out because he didn't fit in with the new principal's philosophy. But the kids all love him, and he's changed many of their lives. That's a big accomplishment around here, where everybody's been doing things the same way for generations, by the book. Would you like to meet him?"

"Yes, I really would."

"Also, there's a young lady who graduated from Tulane. Her name is Rose Phillips. She's an architect, a real sweet kid, wholesome and down to earth. She came from Pennsylvania for college and decided to stay after her graduation. Maybe we could all go out to dinner if you'd like."

"Let's try it. I would enjoy meeting them."

André called and left messages for both of them, telling them to call at a friend's restaurant at a certain time and they would be able to reach him. Surprisingly it worked, and they all met on Bourbon Street at four o'clock.

"Earl, this is Joshua," André said, as he introduced him.

"Yes, I know quite a bit about him, from friends. I had always hoped I would meet him, and I am not at all disappointed. In fact, I am thrilled. Joshua, this is a real joy for me to meet you. It is really the highlight of my life."

"Joshua, this is Rose. Isn't she beautiful?"

"Yes, in more than one way. It is a joy, Rose. How is Maria?"

"Fine, but how do you know my sister?"

And before Joshua got a chance to respond, she continued, "I miss her terribly ever since she left to work in Houston. But I'm happy for her. She likes her work there and she's happy. That's what really matters."

"Earl has been on fire spreading the Good News for the past few years," André broke in. "Some people think he's wonderful, some think he's out in space. But one thing is for sure, he has had a tremendous effect on the kids."

"André's the same way. Joshua. That's why he's so high in his praise of me."

"I think you are all remarkable. I am fortunate to have had a chance to meet you. You make my stay here in New Orleans a happy one."

"How long are you staying?" André asked.

"Perhaps a few days," Joshua responded.

"Do you think you could come and talk to my students?" Earl asked him. "I think you might approve of what you see in them."

"I would be happy to."

"Rose, what kind of architectural work do you do?" Joshua asked.

"Well, our firm does mostly commercial, but the residential is fun, because you know you are helping people prepare a place where they will spend most of their lives, a place they can feel is an expression of themselves. It is much more personal."

"Maybe André will have you build a home for himself and his family."

"André lives in the bayou," Rose replied. "They don't hire architects out there. They just get their friends together and put their own houses up themselves. If we had to depend on them for a living we'd starve. They have a lifestyle all their own. They're very creative and inventive."

André grinned broadly as she was speaking, knowing full well that Cajuns pride themselves on their independence.

"That's true," he said. "We are very self-sufficient. In

fact, my son, Jody, built his own fishing trawler. To buy one would have cost over a quarter of a million dollars. He and his friends built it themselves. And I have to boast; it is one of the nicest boats on the bayou. Or, I should say, it used to be."

"What do you mean, 'it used to be'? Earl asked.

"Well, they had an accident a while back. They were out shrimping one night, and, in the dark, collided with an abandoned offshore oil rig that had no lights on it. The boat was smashed, and my son and crew were tossed into the cold waters of the Gulf. They thought for sure it was the end of their lives. They could see nothing, couldn't even see each other, couldn't call for help, and in the dark couldn't tell which way to shore. All they knew was that they were miles out from land.

"Fortunately, they found the ladders to the deck of the oil rig, and climbed up to the deck where they spent the night. When morning came they located the control room, and managed to get the radio working so they could call the Coast Guard. They came a short time later and rescued them. Thank God, they all survived, though my son was badly injured. By the way, Joshua, now that everyone is inviting you to their place, how about coming out to Bayou La Fourche to meet my family. We will welcome you with a hospitality the likes of which you've never experienced before, gua-*raahn*-teed. And there is no cuisine in the world like Cajun cookin', again, gua-*raahn*-teed."

"And I can imagine there is no humor in the world like Cajun humor, true?" Joshua needled him.

"Gua-*raahn*-teed."

"Well, I can't invite you to my place," Rose remarked, "since my family all live in Pennsylvania, but if you'd like, I would love to show you the office where I work, and some of the work I do."

"Thank you, Rose. I *would* like that very much."

"Well, let's go and have some gumbo soup and po'boy sandwiches," André said, as they approached his favorite café, still in business since his days in college.

When they finished, André said he would be taking Joshua to Bayou La Fourche. Earl protested, saying he'd never be able to visit his classes. André had to give him one of his notorious gua-*raahn*-tees that he would get Joshua back to the city in plenty of time to visit with Earl's students on Monday afternoon.

"Would Tuesday be convenient for you, Rose, since the rest of the time is already accounted for?" Joshua asked her apologetically.

"Tuesday is perfectly all right, Joshua. I'll be expecting you about nine-thirty, if that's not too early."

"I'll be there."

The trip to the bayou was unlike any trip Joshua had ever experienced. The only road to the complex system of inland waterways became more enchanting, and yet more lonely the farther they drove.

"How come your people chose to live so far from the city, and so far out into such an isolated place?" Joshua asked André.

"When they originally came here, they had little choice. Religious persecution drove them from Nova Scotia. If you have ever read 'Evangeline,' Longfellow's poem about the

Acadians, that is our story. Our ancestors came here with nothing. The only way they could make a living was by fishing, and the best place to fish was out here in the bayous. Land was cheap, nobody wanted it. Shrimp were plentiful, and at the time there was little competition. And the people were crafty and industrious, so they built their own homes and their own fishing boats and by living simple lives they made do with what little they had. They even invented their own style of cooking, which is unlike cooking in any place else in the world. Cajuns are famous the world over for their delicious recipes, and spicy seasonings. My wife, Juliette, is the best Cajun cook in La Fourche. Cooking in the city is nothing like my wife's cooking."

"But you grew up in New Orleans. How did you come to live out here?" Joshua asked him.

"Well, that's a long story. I was a priest, or I should say, I am a priest. The archbishop sent me out to Cutoff, the name of the place where my parish was. It was terribly lonely out here all by myself. I took it as long as I could, then I met with the archbishop and told him I couldn't live this way. So I resigned. I met Juliette and fell in love. Shortly afterward I married Juliette and we have had a wonderful life ever since. I think you will like my wife and my family."

"I am sure I will, André. If they have your happy, child-like spirit, they must be delightful people."

When they arrived at André's house, it was late, so they quietly slipped into the house and went directly to bed.

The next morning, André got up early, but not early enough to beat Joshua, who was walking out in front of the house. They made breakfast, which André served Juliette in bed, to her shock and embarrassment, then, finishing their own breakfast, they went out to take a walk down to the dock. But, halfway down the street, they saw André and Juliette's married daughter, Becky, driving back from the creek where she had just dredged up a bushelful of crayfish. As Becky continued on her way to the house, the two men walked back to meet her. Joshua grinned from ear to ear when he saw her emerging from the car. The young woman, dressed in blue jeans with pants legs rolled up, and an old blouse with a few buttons missing, and feet bare, created quite an impression. Besides the appearance of her clothes, her brown curly hair was disheveled, and perspiration was rolling down her cheeks, which she wiped with the inside of her sleeve. She created the image of a strong, earthy woman, well able to care for herself. But when she smiled, a warm beauty shined through appearances that completely changed her image to a beautiful young fun-loving girl who radiated a playful, childlike spirit.

The two walked over to the car. Becky dried her hands on her pants and held a sticky hand out to Joshua. He shook it without wincing.

"Welcome to our home!" she said with a warm smile.

"Thank you."

"Let's go inside and chat with Juliette. I'm sure she's up by now."

As soon as they set foot inside, the most delicious odors filled their senses.

"André, I have never smelled anything so delicious in my

whole life," Joshua exclaimed. "Your wife is an artist. I can't wait to taste whatever it is she is cooking."

At that point Juliette emerged from the living room and entered the kitchen.

"Juliette, this is my friend Joshua. I should have called and told you I was bringing a new friend home, but I knew you wouldn't mind."

"I never know who he's bringing home, but you seem different. You are most welcome," she said as she reached to shake Joshua's hand. "I didn't know he'd brought someone home until I heard the two of you talking this morning. I was embarrassed when André served my breakfast in bed; especially knowing there was a stranger in the kitchen. Well, André's timing was good this time," she said, "because I'm cooking everybody's favorite, pork and gravy, Cajun style."

Juliette was more businesslike and efficient than the rest of the family. Someone had to be. It was easy to tell she carried most of the family burdens, as André's genius for making friends and counseling them was of little help around the house. Though no longer active as a priest, he was still the most active priest in the bayou. Most of the people went to him with their problems because of his caring, compassionate heart.

Joshua watched the interplay of the family's personalities, and noticed the warmth of their feelings for one another. Though they needled each other in their conversations, it was done with affection.

"Joshua, come into the living room where we can talk and get out of the women's way. There's too much going on there and it makes me nervous, otherwise we'll end up working."

"That's all right. I don't mind helping. If we're going to eat we should share the work, too."

"You tell him, Joshua. He always knows just when to disappear," Juliette said to them as they left the kitchen.

"Juliette, I help you all the time, but you end up throwing me out of the kitchen because I get in your way," André said in his defense. The statement was only half-true. André knew just how to be a nuisance and get in the way. "Besides, darlin'," he continued, "you always do your best cooking when I'm not around to distract you."

"André, you distract me whether you're around or not."

"Oh, you say the nicest things. After all these years I still distract you."

"Not in the way you're thinking."

"It sounded nice anyway. I'd better quit while I'm ahead," André concluded.

"Your wife has to be a very patient woman, André," Joshua commented.

"She is that. She has to be with me, because I guess I'm more like one of the kids in her mind. Thank God she still loves me. She is a wonderful woman, and each day I appreciate her more and more. Oh, by the way, tonight is our prayer group time. I hope you don't mind the gang coming over. It's a fun night. They all have their problems, which we discuss and pray over, but T-Boy brings his trumpet and we have music like, I gua-*raahn*-tee, you never heard before."

"That should be enjoyable."

After only a few minutes, André decided to take Joshua down to the wharf, which they'd started out for in the first place.

"Darlin', we'll be back in about an hour. We're going down to see Jody and his friends at the dock."

"Lunch will be ready at noon," she said, knowing full well that they would not be back in an hour.

The wharf was filled with fishing boats of all kinds, some purchased, some homemade. Some were just coming in after being out all night. Some were tied up, and would be going out later in the day to come back tomorrow with their catch.

"See that large boat over there, the third one down. The young fellow standing there in white pants, that's Jody, Juliette's son. He's the one I was telling you about yesterday."

"Jody," André said, as they walked up the plank, "this is my friend, Joshua. I've told him all about you."

"*All* about me?"

"Well, not exactly, but enough. I met Joshua in the city a few days ago. He was wandering around and didn't know anybody, so we became friends. I told him all about your boat and how we're lucky you're still with us. Could you show Joshua around your friend's boat?"

"Sure, nice to meet you, Joshua. If you come over here, I'll show you inside the cabin."

The three went inside. It was impressive. Large enough for the pilot and six or seven crew members, with four berths on either side of the cabin. A refrigerator, a stove, and other appliances made it possible to spend days at sea in relative comfort. Joshua was impressed, especially when he was told that Jody and his friend built the boat all by themselves, just by following plans they had been given by another friend.

After emerging from the boat, they walked along the dock, meeting fishermen as they went along. Fishermen today are not much different from fishermen of centuries ago, Joshua noticed. They had the same earthy mannerisms, the same blunt honesty and forthrightness that he found and loved so much in the apostles. They were no-nonsense people. The harshness of the life molded them that way.

"It's too bad we can't take Joshua out for a fishing trip," André said to Jody.

Jody thought for a minute and called a few of his buddies together. After a brief discussion, Jody came over to his father, and with a broad smile, said, "Okay, André, let's get into the boat. A couple of the men will come with us, but they have to call their wives first to tell them they are going out trawling for a while.

"Now, this is going to be a real fishing trip. I don't know whether we will have any luck with the shrimp. Sometimes, even after being out all night we come home with nothing. But we'll see. I told my friend earlier I might take his boat out, and he didn't mind as he wasn't going to use it anyway."

Leaving the dock, they slowly motored down the channel. In a few minutes they were in the Gulf. Turning on the radar, Jody hoped he would spot a shrimp bed, but to no avail. After almost an hour, he was ready to give up.

"Jody, take the boat about a thousand feet to starboard, and let down your nets," Joshua told him.

Jody was reluctant to do as Joshua directed, but unwilling to offend his father's friend, he decided there was nothing to lose, and did as he said. Arriving at the spot, Joshua said, "This is it, just about forty, maybe fifty feet more, and let down the nets."

Jody felt foolish just dropping the nets in a place at random. It was so unscientific. But he did it anyway.

The crew dropped the net, and began to drag it. There seemed to be a pull, but it was probably a large piece of coral, or the ruins of an old boat. But the pull was steady and kept getting heavier. There definitely was something alive in the net. The farther they went, the heavier the tug on the net. Finally, the men decided to haul the net on board to see what they had dragged up.

To their astonishment, the net was filled with shrimp, at least a ton, worth a small fortune. They all yelled with wild excitement. Joshua stood there watching them as if they were little children. Just like the apostles the morning after they had toiled the whole night and caught nothing.

"Joshua, how did you know there would be shrimp there?" Jody asked, as he hugged him with his powerful arms. The others brought the catch on board.

Joshua said nothing, just smiled.

They motored back to shore to the shouts of the crew and their friends on the dock. No one could believe they'd gone out there and caught a ton of shrimp so fast. But there it was.

Jody called his friend who owned the boat and told him the news. He was down on the dock in no time at all.

"We're rich! We're rich!" he screamed with the others, as they danced along the dock. "And look at the size of them. They're super jumbos."

Joshua was the hero of the day.

Needless to say, André and Joshua missed lunch, but Juliette was used to that. Without any fuss, she and Becky and Becky's son, Julian, ate without them. When they came in two hours later, lunch was all ready and waiting for them on the stove.

"Juliette!" André called, as he shoved open the screen door. "Juliette, you will never believe what happened today," as he went on to relate the whole episode. Even she found it hard to believe, and thought her husband was either making up the story or exaggerating. She knew how many hours her son spent dragging the bottom of the Gulf hoping they would find a catch to justify all their time and hard work.

"No, it's true, it's really true. I'm not even exaggerating."

When she looked at Joshua, she got no help from him. In fact he seemed so uninterested, she was more convinced than ever that her husband was making up the story. She went back to scooping the crayfish out of the boiling water, and putting them into a huge pot.

Since he was getting nowhere, André changed the subject. "Honey, the cooking smells delicious."

"I hope I get a chance to taste it," Joshua said.

"You will if my husband doesn't disappear with you again."

André pulled off a piece of bread from a freshly baked loaf, dipped it in the gravy, and gave it to Joshua. Sheepishly he took it and ate it, with a look of great delight on his face. Then André did the same for himself.

"Would you two mind helping me with these crayfish?

They're a nuisance to prepare, but if you all want gumbo, you have to help. I'll never finish by myself, and Becky had things to do."

"No, we'd be glad to," Joshua said with a grin, while André grimaced. "Trapped again," he muttered.

For the next hour and a half they shelled crayfish and prepared them for Juliette to use for Sunday dinner.

By that time it was almost five o'clock.

"Well, we're finally finished. Joshua and I are going to walk down the lane and say hello to some of the neighbors. We'll be back in time for supper."

"Don't be too long. We'll be eating in an hour."

It wasn't long before Juliette was ready with the dinner. She rang the bell on the porch to call everyone to the table. André and Joshua surprised her and came back on time. Sitting around the table were Becky, Juliette, Jody, Julian, André, and Joshua.

"André, would you say the grace?" Juliette asked.

"Dear Father in heaven, our little family is gathered around the table once again. We thank you for that, Lord, first of all. We are honored to have a guest with us today, Lord. We see in him you yourself, Lord, whom we have welcomed into our home. Bless his stay among us and bless this food which we are about to eat, and bless our dear Juliette, who always seasons her food with love. We ask this as always in Jesus' name."

"Amen," everyone responded.

"I don't think I could have waited much longer to eat, with that delicious odor floating all around the house," Joshua remarked.

"It is delicious," Joshua said, after tasting his first bite.

Jody was a quiet young man, tall and well built, with a powerful physique, and thick black hair. Like his mother, he was reserved and pensive. Joshua noticed how he was attentive to everyone at the table, and passed the food as someone was ready for a second helping.

"Jody, how have you been feeling since the accident?" Joshua asked him.

"My back hurts a lot, and I still have headaches, something I never had before. I just hope someday it will all go away."

"Jody hasn't been able to work ever since the accident. He's been in constant pain, but he never complains," André added.

"I hope someday I get better, so I can work again. I don't like just sitting around or walking the docks talking to all my friends as they mend their nets and tend their boats. Even today I felt bad not helping the crew pulling the shrimp on board."

"But it is not a waste," Joshua told him. "You are learning things now, and growing in ways you never imagined. The understanding of life you develop now will enrich you. Many others, as well, will be blessed in the future by the wisdom and understanding you are developing. So, do not be discouraged. Good times are fun, but we learn most and grow strongest from our pain. You will find that these difficult days are the most productive period of your life, a time in which you can grow more than at any other time."

"I don't feel like I'm growing. I just feel weary. I've always worked and I don't like sitting around doing nothing,"

Jody answered. "Joshua, I had the strangest feeling this morning when you told the crew to cast the net over to starboard side, and just precisely where to cast it. I had the eerie feeling I was living out a gospel story, but in real life. Then we came up with the huge catch of shrimp. Wow, I was convinced."

He said no more. When Juliette heard her son talking about the incident, her curiosity was aroused.

"It really happened?" she asked.

"Yes, Mother," Jody replied.

"I thought André was making up the story, when he told me earlier."

"No, it really happened," her son continued. "There were so many shrimp, I thought for sure the net would break, just like in the gospel story. There was well over a ton of shrimp, jumbos, big jumbos. Everyone was thrilled and the boat wasn't even scheduled to go out until this afternoon. But we just went out to give Joshua a thrill. He ended up giving us the thrill. Everyone's talking about it down at the dock. There's over fifteen thousand dollars' worth of shrimp in that catch."

"Becky, it is not hard to tell who Grandpa's good friend is," Joshua said as he was watching Julian move closer to André.

"No, André is his constant companion. I think he'd rather stay here than come home," she replied.

"Grandpa's my best friend. We take walks together and he teaches me all kinds of things, and we play games and have a lot of fun," Julian said.

After supper, the prayer group assembled. There were

nine in all who came that night, mostly men. As they gathered in the living room, André introduced them to Joshua. After chatting for a while they began their session. Each discussed things that happened during the week; some things were good, some heart-rending. Joshua just listened. One man had just lost his mother. He was a big burly man, with a build like one would imagine Peter the apostle had.

"This was a tough week," the man said. His name was Louis. "I never knew how much Momma meant to me. She was always there. Never asked for anything, was just there for all of us when we needed her, and now she's gone. The house is so empty. I feel like an orphan." He then began to cry, unashamedly. Cajuns, even grown men, are not ashamed to express their feelings.

T-Boy Chereamie, the trumpet player, picked up his trumpet, and said, "This calls for a song for Momma. She was not only Louis' momma. She was a momma to all of us at one time or other." He then began to play. Never had anyone heard a trumpet played the way that man played. The feeling, the emotion, the tender sounds coming forth from an instrument that is usually associated with ear-shattering sounds. Before long everyone was in tears. That to the prayer group was their way of praying. They prayed with their heart and soul, and prayer for them was always an emotional experience. They were really talking to Daddy. Even Joshua was moved to tears by the experience. When they prayed sometimes it was in words, sometimes in music, and sometimes just in silence, when no one could think of anything to say, which wasn't very often.

Joshua remained silent during the meeting. Toward the

end, André asked if Joshua would like to share some of his thoughts with the group, to which he readily assented.

"I have visited many Christian families. Each has its own spirit. Some are quite formal. Many center their gatherings around scripture. The concentration was on the meaning of verses, and how they applied to their personal lives, but Jesus was not real to them, only a distant figure. Another group in Australia gathered people together with Jesus as the center. The leader, a good man named Peter, inspires the people to care for one another as friends, to share each other's joys and pain. Scripture is not a formal part of their gatherings, but Jesus is very present to each of them. This is what I see among you. I had heard about you long ago, and that you were filled with the Holy Spirit. I was hoping that I could one day meet you. Now that I have seen with my own eyes, I am happy at what I see. Jesus is very real to you. If he were physically present here now, you wouldn't open the Bible and start reading scripture. You would celebrate and talk to him and this is just what you do. You celebrate the presence of a real living Jesus in your midst. This is the way Christians should be, joyful people, even in their sorrow, ever celebrating the presence of Jesus. When you were praying, it was simple and natural, pleadings from deep within, especially when you prayed through music. I know my Father listened to your prayer, because he likes music, especially music that comes from the heart, feelings expressed in mournful or happy sounds. I'm sure my Father never misses an evening when you gather to pray.

"As you talked and prayed, I noticed not one of you expressed any concern about the new millennium."

"We talk about it in passing," one man said, "but we never make a big thing about it. Our church never has much to say about these times. The priest may mention it, but not in a way that scares people. He said that most of the prophecies have already taken place, and that the only End Time we have to worry about is the time when we die. We are taught to love God and not be afraid of Him. He is our Daddy, and what Daddy would play such dirty tricks on his kids the way many people expect God to do in the Last Days. God loves us and we know He will always take care of us, and we never have to worry."

"You have a good spirit, the kind of happy, wholesome spirit my Father desires for everyone. It is the true spirit of religion. May you never lose it."

As the meeting ended, people spent a few minutes talking to Joshua, telling him how they appreciated his comments. After they left, Joshua, Juliette, and André sat at the table reminiscing about the meeting, and talking of church affairs.

"Juliette works for the parish," André commented, "and can accept all that goes on in the Church. I will always have a hard time with it, because they are out of touch with the people. They are supposed to be shepherds and servants of God's people. I have seen that in very, very few. Even this present pope; I'm sure he's a good man, even a holy man. He certainly has great courage, and is not afraid to speak his mind. But he lives in a world that is not the world we live in. People respect him and what he stands for, but he's out of touch with people's needs. I know the Church is not a democracy, but grace builds on nature, and the Church has to listen to the people's pain and concerns. That's not democracy. It is just plain courtesy. If they continue to be arrogant, people will respect the pope but won't pay any attention to what he says."

Joshua listened and said nothing until André finished. "André, you are right. There must be sensitivity to people's pain. Where that is lacking in shepherds, people become hurt and drift away into dangerous places, or start their own little communities, which is not good. John Paul was a good shepherd, a strong man, with strong convictions. He needed to be that way in his country. As pope he had to face many difficult problems. One was with theologians whose faith was shallow. Their teachings had strayed and they were confusing people and leading them astray. The guidelines he laid down were necessary at the time. Now things will change. A new shepherd will have the gentleness of Jesus, and bring back many of the wandering sheep. People will listen to him because they will know he understands and cares."

Hardly had Joshua finished speaking when a special news report flashed over the television announcing the death of the pope. André and Juliette were stunned. They looked at Joshua in disbelief. The coincidence of Joshua's words was not lost on them.

"CNN has just received word from its Rome correspondent that the Holy Father, Pope John Paul II, died peacefully in his sleep at two-thirty A.M., Rome time." According to Vatican sources, "The pope had been suffering from a debilitating illness for the last few years and his death did not come as a great surprise to those who were close to him. Funeral arrangements will be announced momentarily. Cardinals, bishops, and archbishops, as well as heads of state and ambassadors will be coming from all over the world to attend the services. They will come to pay their last respects to a man whom the world came to admire. Even those who did not agree with his ideas still had great respect for this man who perhaps more than any other world leader shaped the course of modern political life. It was through his extraordinary political skills and his network of powerful contacts that communism has been dismantled and a new world order has emerged.

"After the funeral services, cardinals from all parts of the world will convene to elect a new pope. As further developments unfold, we will keep our viewers informed."

André looked at Joshua with a quizzical glance. "Isn't it strange that we were talking about the pope and then it's announced that he just died? What a coincidence! So many unusual things have been happening lately, it makes a person wonder whether all these prophecies about the end of the world are true," he continued.

"When weren't there unusual things happening, André? Be realistic! God doesn't work in bizarre ways. God is rational. Why would He cause earthquakes and calamities to announce himself? He doesn't need melodrama to announce His Presence. He works in silence and in hidden ways. His Presence is hardly felt."

"But what about in the Hebrew scriptures, where there were all kinds of dramas surrounding God?"

"Most of those accounts were embellished by storytellers. As the stories were passed down from generation to generation around campfires, they were expanded upon. Also, remember, whenever anything happened in nature, to those simple people, it was always God who did it. It was the way people thought, and even today many people think that way.

"The real prophets understood God, and that He works ordinarily in quiet, subtle ways, not in loud, noisy productions. Elijah heard Him in the gentle breeze."

"Joshua's right. People still think that way. When something tragic happens, people wonder if it isn't a punishment from God," Juliette commented, then asked, "Joshua, we're going to have the whole family over tomorrow. Are you going to be here, or is André bringing you back to the city?"

"I think we're staying here till after dinner tomorrow. How could we miss your Sunday dinner, after all the raving André does about your cooking?"

"I was hoping you'd stay. We have something special every Sunday, to honor the Lord."

"If today's meal wasn't special, I can't begin to imagine what tomorrow's will be like," Joshua commented.

It was late, past midnight, and everyone was tired. André showed Joshua to his room. They all slept well.

CHAPTER 13

EVEN BEFORE THE pope died, people were maneuvering in an attempt to influence the election of the next pope. The deceased pope was a good man, but rigidly conservative. Having spent his life first under Nazi domination, then under communism, he was not conditioned toward liberalism. As bishop, then archbishop, then cardinal, he was leader of the Church in Poland, a country where there were few Protestants to stimulate interest in ecumenical togetherness. It was a monolithic Church, a Church whose power was in its solidarity and unity of faith and purpose. The purpose was to preserve the faith of the people, especially the young, against the onslaughts of an atheistic state. "Never compromise!" was their battle cry, burnt into their hearts from their youth.

When Karol Wojtyla became pope, his conditioning of a

lifetime did not change. As pope he was still concerned about people's faith being diluted and watered down by the onslaught of a liberalism in theology that was even more dangerous, in his mind, than communism. Though generally respected and loved by many, his rigidly conservative proclamations and regulations were looked upon as regressive, oppressive, and offensive to the Christian freedom of spirit. The worldwide movements toward Christian unity were stifled. Newly ordained bishops and priests were not only conservative, which in itself can be a good trait in a leader, but concerned more with the strict imposition of law than with the pain and loneliness so many people today were suffering. As a result hundreds of thousands of people left the Church because they or members of their family were denied the sacraments, often in violation of Church law, or treated harshly by a priest. A mean spirit seemed to take hold throughout the Church, a spirit that was intolerant of any thought and belief different from their own. This mean-spiritedness did much to destroy the camaraderie that so wonderfully characterized the previous generation of priests.

Now that the election of a new pontiff was imminent, powerful groups of every persuasion were working frantically behind the scenes in desperate attempts to influence the outcome of the election. One very wealthy group in particular, more faithful to the Council of Trent in the sixteenth century than to the recent teachings of the Church, which they considered suspect, was notorious for its generous gifts to important cardinals working in the Vatican. This group had the most to lose if their candidate was not elected, because they were not well thought of by the more open-minded members of the hierarchy. They had a reputation for being devious and underhanded in the way they operated within the Church. Now was the time for this organization to cash in its chips and remind its dependents of their obligations, which it was not shy about doing.

At the same time, liberal groups were organizing influential members to exert pressure on their friends among the cardinal electors. It was a quiet drama, taking place during the days following the death of the pope, often in restaurants where they could casually meet for supper or over cappuccino and pastry. There is not supposed to be politicking before the election of a pope, but who can prevent it, even among the cardinals themselves who are most concerned about the future direction of the Church?

When the time for the conclave finally arrived, the cardinals went in procession to the Sistine Chapel and were properly directed to their cubicles where they would reside in total isolation, not only from the outside world but from each other, until they elected a new pope. There would be two *scrutini,* or ballots, each day until a simple majority would finally elect a successor to St. Peter.

This election took longer than usual. It lasted almost four tantalizing days. Conservatives who had a strong caucus in the College of Cardinals were well organized and determined to preserve the status quo established by the now deceased pope. Those with a more forward-looking vision had a number of good men to choose from but had never tried to predetermine the election before the assembly began.

The balloting on the morning of the first day found the votes spread among a host of candidates.

The crowd waiting impatiently in the piazza was disappointed when a wisp of dark smoke floated up from the little chimney over the Sistine Chapel.

On the second ballot that afternoon, the numbers narrowed considerably, with the conservative candidate in a strong position. Black smoke again sent another disappointing message. On the second day, the balloting in the morning saw a hardening of positions, with the conservative, a German cardinal by the name of Christoph Larbisch, holding a solid block of thirty votes. A cardinal from northern Italy, Francesco Montarini, split seventy votes with a cardinal from Africa named Isaiah Muchina. The remaining twenty-five or so votes were scattered among three other cardinals, one from Japan, another from India, and a third from Brazil.

The afternoon ballot saw little change, except the Indian candidate dropped out and his votes went to Cardinal Larbisch, giving him a total of forty-six votes, with Cardinal Montarini picking up three more votes, giving him a total of thirty-eight. Cardinal Muchina lost six votes, giving him twenty-nine votes, with the other two splitting the remainder.

The balloting on the morning of the third day was practically identical with that of the day before. Still black smoke, with the people wondering why it was taking so long. There were all kinds of rumors. The afternoon ballot set the stage for a showdown among Cardinal Montarini, Cardinal Larbisch, and Cardinal Muchina, when the cardinals from Japan and Brazil received no votes. Cardinal Muchina picked up six votes, giving him a total of thirty-five votes.

Cardinal Larbisch now had forty-seven votes and Cardinal Montarini forty-one votes.

Again, the huge crowd in the piazza was disappointed when they saw the black smoke emerge from the chimney. The cardinals themselves were weary. Unable to discuss their feelings and convictions with one another they were forced to depend on their prayers that the Holy Spirit would guide their final choice, and elect a pope after God's wishes, and not theirs.

The balloting on the morning of the fourth day saw a dramatic change in favor of Cardinal Larbisch. He received ten votes when Cardinal Muchina's supporters began to waver. On this ballot he received only twenty-five votes. With ten going to Larbisch, the remaining votes went to Montarini, who now had forty-four votes, with Larbisch having a total of fifty-seven votes. It now looked as if the conservatives who had voted for Muchina were afraid that Montarini would pick up more votes, so they instinctively switched and gave their votes to Larbisch.

The afternoon balloting would tell the tale. It was hard to see how Cardinal Larbisch could lose, but no one knew the thoughts of the remaining supporters of Cardinal Muchina. When the balloting started, one vote after another went to Cardinal Larbisch. Occasionally, Cardinal Montarini would receive a vote. Halfway through the counting, Cardinal Larbisch had fifty-nine votes, and Cardinal Montarini had fifty. Then, one vote after another went to Cardinal Montarini, until he had sixty votes and Cardinal Larbisch had sixty-one votes. The final four votes went as follows, Cardinal Larbisch, Cardinal Montarini, Cardinal Montarini, Cardinal Montarini. Cardinal Montarini had been elected pope.

Would he accept was the next question. The eyes of all the cardinals were on him. He sat there with his head in his hands. When asked if he accepted his election, he lowered his hands. Everyone could see he was crying. After a few moments, to gain his composure, he looked up and said, "Yes, if this is what God wants, I accept."

"I assure you, Francesco," the presiding cardinal whispered, "from the bottom of my heart, this is what God wants. The Holy Spirit has called you."

"Then, I accept the election."

"What name do you take?"

"Christoforo, the Christ-bearer. We must bring him back to the people."

"My brothers, Cardinal Montarini has accepted. We now have a new Holy Father." The cardinals applauded, some loudly, some halfheartedly. They then paid their formal respects to the new pope.

Within minutes the fire was started, sending white smoke up the chimney. The crowd in the piazza, which had swelled in numbers as the days passed, went wild when they realized a pope had been elected.

"Who is it, who is it?" they kept asking one another as if someone in the crowd knew. In a short time the new pope would be dressed in papal robes and led to the balcony of St. Peter's basilica, where he would be introduced to the people.

All eyes were on the balcony overlooking the vast piazza.

When the door to the balcony finally opened almost an hour later, a thunderous applause burst out, and became even greater when a figure appeared, not that of the pope, but of the cardinal deacon. He motioned for silence, and surprisingly, within a few seconds an uncanny silence settled over the huge crowd.

"Habemus papam! We have a pope. His name is Francesco." Before he finished announcing his last name, the crowd again went wild. "Montarini, Montarini," they screamed. The whole world was praying, they thought against hope, that he would be elected.

"Francesco Montarini," the cardinal deacon continued. "The Holy Father has taken the name of Christopher I." He then led the pope to the balcony. When they saw in papal robes the one they hoped and prayed for, the crowd's joy was beyond control. The pope stood there, humbly accepting their warm show of affection, and waited until they quieted down.

"My dear friends," he started out saying, "I thank you all for coming here today to pray for the Church and for its leaders that we be responsive to the Holy Spirit. I always believed the Holy Spirit does not make mistakes, but today, after my being chosen as pope, I now wonder. Only time will tell if He made a mistake. In my heart I never thought or believed that this would happen to me. And, looking at myself in the mirror as I dressed in these robes, I had to laugh at how funny I looked, but then I cried in disbelief. The responsibilities of the pope are monumental. I know that I by myself will never be equal to the task. I pray and ask you to pray that God will give me the grace to be an instrument of

His will for the Church, so the Church, which is you and me and all of us together, will be able to follow the lead of the Good Shepherd.

"I know you are surprised that I took the name Christopher. As you know it means 'Christ-bearer.' I want to bring Jesus back to a world, yes, even a Christian world, that has all but forgotten him. I want also to make a statement that each of us must be a Christ-bearer in our world that is beset with so much hatred and so many complex problems. It is important for all of us to refocus our sights on the One Person who alone as the Light of the World can guide our feet in the way of peace and freedom.

"Too many people feel alienated from God's family. Too many people walk this earth lonely and unloved. Too many people die, not from sickness, not from starvation, not from disease, but from lack of love. That should not be. No one should ever have to live his or her life deprived of love. That is why God sent His Son, to bring love into the world. In fidelity to that mission of the Savior, I wish to be a good shepherd, seeking out the bruised, the crippled, the hurting, and lonely sheep. I would like to invite them back home, to take their rightful places at the table of the Lord. I would also like to offer to the whole world an invitation to open their minds and hearts to Jesus, and ask if they might consider the message of Jesus as the solution to the major problems of the world. These problems are too vast and complex for the human mind alone to comprehend, much less to solve.

"I want Christians everywhere to know that I am, first and foremost, the Bishop of the Diocese of Rome. To emphasize this my first step will be to live among the people. As soon as it is feasible I will take up residence at the Church of San Giovanni in Laterano, which as every Roman knows, has been the seat of the Bishop of Rome since the earliest centuries of Christianity. With regard to other bishops, I look upon all bishops as successors of the apostles, and would like them to take their rightful place in the Church, by my side, a place which has been denied them for too long a time. Together, as Jesus intended, we will guide the Church throughout the world. The Vatican staff will be our service team, to carry out decisions we as bishops have made. As successor to Peter, and entrusted with the keys to the kingdom, I will try, as Jesus instructed Peter, to be a faithful guide and support to my fellow apostles, and to confirm their faith when necessary. In short, I would like to be, first to bishops and priests, then, to all of you, nothing more than the Servant of the servants of God. And now may I ask God's blessing on each of you here and on your families, and on the whole world." The pope then chanted, *"Benedictio Dei omnipotentis, Patris et Filii, et Spiritus Sancti descendat super vos and maneat semper.* [May the blessing of Almighty God, the Father, Son, and Holy Spirit descend upon you and be with you forever.]"

The vast throng sang in one thunderous voice, "Amen."

ON SUNDAY, JOSHUA enjoyed the dinner with André and Juliette's family. He and André left early to get back to New Orleans at a reasonable time, so Joshua could spend time with Earl. André had called Earl earlier and told him they would be at his house at seven o'clock. He was thrilled.

The evening went fast, too fast, when there was so much to discuss. Earl had been teaching for years, and had the rare ability to stir up his young students to make a difference in life around them. He made Jesus real for the kids, and in making Jesus real, he came alive in their hearts. They couldn't wait to bring Jesus into the community with them. Occasionally, however, some parents became suspicious that their teenager should be so fired up for Christ. Why couldn't he just learn their faith and be like everybody else? What's up with this teacher?

Then the phone calls would start, and the inevitable investigations into what this radical teacher was teaching the kids. Rather than being happy their children had fallen in love with God, they were threatened that their children should be so religious. Having lost his job in one school, Earl couldn't afford to lose another job, especially since he had a family to support. Yet, he knew this was the only real way to teach religion. Teach them about Jesus. Isn't that what it's all about? After all he is our religion. What should be so frightening about a young student falling in love with God?

Early next morning Earl dropped Joshua off at Rose's office so she could spend a few minutes with him. After introducing him to her boss, she brought him into a conference room and showed him some of her work: sketches, watercolor renderings, and Styrofoam models of various buildings she was working on. For such a young woman, she had accomplished much in her few years.

"Your work has a lot of feeling, Rose. You create spaces that are warm and friendly, places where people can enjoy spending time, even when it is workspace."

Since Rose's office was a busy place, Joshua spent only a few minutes there. But before he took his leave, he left Rose with a suggestion for her boss. "On the other side of town, there is a very large piece of land that the federal government is willing to give away to a developer. However, the developer must be willing to construct a model village for people of limited means, a self-contained village with schools, offices, stores, and recreation centers, and the people presently living there now must be employed on the construction jobs. The government will also provide generous financing and make available worthwhile tax credit. Share it with your employer, Rose. It will be well worth his while to consider it."

"Joshua, how do you know that?" she asked.

"Just check into it, and you will see."

Joshua walked through parts of the city, talking to people, sensing their pain, and encouraging them with his rare insight into their future, and the good things that would happen if they did not lose hope.

After lunch he arrived at Earl's school. The students were about to start their classes. Earl thought it only proper that he first introduce Joshua to the principal, before bringing him into his classroom. The principal was gracious enough, but having already had phone calls from some of the parents about Earl's unusual class techniques, he was suspicious as to how this visitor would be received, and what would be the consequences when news of it reached the parents. The principal had been trying to protect Earl from some parents who were forever finding fault.

"John, this is Joshua. We are good friends, and I would like my class to meet him. He is widely traveled and has a beautiful message."

"What kind of a message does he intend to share with the students?" the principal asked.

"If you think I'm on fire for Jesus, this man really has it."

At that point, a man, having heard that someone named Joshua was going to speak to the students, came bursting into the principal's office. He was beside himself with rage.

"Why do you let this man in the school? Why do you let

him come to disturb the children? Leave them alone. The children are all right the way they are."

Joshua looked at the man. He turned and looked at Joshua. It was a look of deepest hatred. "You don't fool me. I know who you are. You have come here to destroy us all."

The principal, who was a peaceable man, could not understand what was happening. The whole incident was unnerving. He knew the man from the neighborhood, but no one paid much attention to him. He had once been a brilliant teacher at a university, but then he became odd, and people began to shun him. Rumor had it that certain people in the community, some very intelligent, would meet with him regularly, and strange religious rites would take place.

When Joshua looked at the creature, the man's face became contorted with hatred. "Why did you come here? Why don't you leave us alone? We were all happy here before you came. This city has been a haven for us for many years."

"Be silent, and leave the man in peace," Joshua commanded.

At that the figure looked at Joshua as if pleading for pity, then cringed and began to convulse violently, falling to the floor as if dead.

"My God, what's going on?" the principal said.

"Don't worry, he'll be all right," Joshua said, to reassure the two men.

The prostrate figure began to move slowly, looked up, embarrassed and ashamed. Joshua took him by the hand and lifted him up, but it was obvious he was very weak. Looking at Joshua, he began to weep.

"Thank you, Lord. I am so grateful. That hideous being

has possessed me for many years. I was helpless to free myself. The shame, the humiliation, was more than I could bear. I had often thought of destroying myself to get rid of them; there were many of them, you know, but somehow, I knew that that would be wrong, so I endured it all these years. I am so grateful for what you have done for me."

"You are a child of God, Matthew," Joshua said to him. "What has happened to you has stripped you of all your pride as a young man, which made you easy prey to those creatures. But you are now free. Go back home to your mother. She has been praying for you all these years. She will be happy to see you healed and free again."

The man reached out, took Joshua's hand, and kissed it, then with tears of joy and gratitude, turned and walked out of the building.

Earl and the principal stood there speechless.

"What was that all about?" Earl asked Joshua.

"It is something people today do not witness very often," Joshua told them. "Long ago that man fell victim to his own pride, pride in his great intelligence. As a result he was a very lonely man. Dry and deserted souls like that are an easy prey for the evil one, who, without much difficulty, entered into him and took possession of him."

"You mean that was really the devil?" the principal asked, dumbfounded.

"Yes, it was not the man speaking, but the evil one using the man's voice."

"He said he knew you. How does he know you?" the principal continued.

"Evil is always threatened by my presence, and reacts the same way, partly in arrogance, as if to threaten me, partly in fear for what I might do. Evil is always confused in the presence of Goodness."

"Who are you?" the principal pressed him further.

"I am Joshua."

"How do you know so much about the evil one, as you call him?" the principal asked.

"I have known Satan from long ago."

Not knowing where to go from there, the principal let up on his questioning.

"Well, I am pleased to meet you, Joshua, I think. I hope you enjoy your visit to our school. I also hope you enjoy your visit to Earl's class. I would appreciate it if you would be discreet in what you have to say to the students. Some of the parents are very touchy about what is discussed in class, as Earl can tell you, I am sure."

The two men shook hands and Earl conducted Joshua to his classroom. On the way down the corridor, Earl said to him, "Joshua, I thought I knew a lot about you from my friends, and from books, but in real life, 'You rule, man, you rule!' as the kids say."

As the two approached the classroom, students walking past looked, wondering, and smiled at Joshua, as if they already knew him. When they entered the classroom, the students became quiet, and looked at Earl. From his look they knew they were in for a surprise.

Earl started the class with customary prayer. Everyone sat down.

"Remember, class, I promised you a treat some day? Well, we are getting more of a treat than even I expected. I am honored to introduce to you today . . . Joshua."

"No way, man. No way," one boy said, unbelieving.

The rest of the class sat silently, in disbelief.

"Here, I've been telling them about you all this time and now that you are here with them, they just sit there with not a word to say. I don't believe it."

"Are you really Joshua?" another boy asked.

"Yes, that is my name."

"The real Joshua?"

"Don't I look real?"

"Yeah, but what I mean is, well, you know what I mean."

"If you're really Joshua, why would you want to come and visit us. We're nobody."

"That's the kind of people I have always liked. People who think they are somebody always gave me trouble. And why would you be surprised that I would visit you. Don't you know that I am always with you? Many years ago, there was a good and holy king. His name was King Louis of France. One day while Mass was being offered in the palace chapel, at the consecration time, Jesus appeared at the altar. Everyone was shocked. One of the courtiers ran upstairs, breathless, to the King's chambers.

" 'Your Majesty, Your Majesty,' he said. 'Come quickly, Jesus just appeared at the altar at consecration time. Come quickly so you can see him.'

" 'Go back down, my son,' the King replied. 'It is not

necessary for me to go down to see him. I always knew he was there.'

"Why do you find it difficult to believe that I would come to visit you? I am with you always. I am only too happy to visit you today. After all, how many students learn about me in their classes? There are many who study the Bible and who study theology, but few who learn about me. You are among the few, so I am very happy to be here with you."

"Joshua, is God angry and upset over all the hatred and meanness in the world?" a girl asked.

"You must always remember God is not a human being. God does not get angry. Anger happens when a person loses control over what is happening. God never loses control over His creation. God does feel sadness over the pain people endure. It is, however, not the kind of sadness you may feel. When a human being feels sad, it is because someone or something important has been injured or destroyed. God is sad because He shares people's pain. God does not cause pain. People bring that on themselves and others."

"Why doesn't God do something about it then?" another girl asked.

"Remember, God gives everyone free will. That is an awesome privilege, which we thought over for a long moment, because we saw every evil thing it would bring about. But in the end we decided that people had to be free in order to love. My Father created people to love because that was the only way they could enter heaven and share our life, by choosing to enter into our love. That is why love is the only test of a person's goodness. It is not the law that makes a person pleasing in my Father's eyes, but the love a person has in his or her heart. A person who loves will keep God's law because it tells people to treat God and all His creatures with respect. But love goes far beyond that. Love inspires a person to give over and above what is demanded by law, and to share one's gifts and treasures with others who have little and who are hurting.

"God is not pleased by all the evil in the world. But God sees far beyond the evil. He understands the pain and anguish of soul that drives a person to do evil things. Strangely, God even feels the pain of evil people but they resist His continual prodding to change their hearts.

"God, however, feels most sad over those people who suffer most from others' meanness and hatred. He is closer to those people than they could ever begin to imagine. This is hard for human beings to imagine, but God, in His immensity, sees everything in creation as what would be microscopic to you. A thousand years to God is like a fleeting second to you. When God sees a person in pain, though he does not always interfere in the course of nature, and take away his pain, he knows that one day when He takes that person home, he or she will have a reward that is far beyond anything the human mind could imagine. The suffering one endures here to a great extent will determine the joy a person will experience in heaven. Remember, God is a just God."

"Joshua, do evil people go to hell?" a girl asked.

"Even though we talk about people being evil, there is no such thing as an evil person. My Father does not create evil people. People do evil things because of the pain and inner torture they have experienced in life. Not everyone has the strength of character to rise above the meanness and injustice and lack of love in their life. In their unresolved anger, which turns to hatred, they do evil things. They may choose never to love, and to be completely selfish, and do horribly evil things to others. If they die that way, where should they go?"

"To hell?" a boy asked.

"Sometimes, before they die, God gives them a vision of all the pain and evil they have caused, and if there is any goodness left in them, they shrink in terror from what they see in themselves. I cannot describe the pain these people feel when God lets them see themselves as He sees them, and all the evil they have done to others. That is the final grace He offers to them. If they accept that grace and repent, God in His mercy shows compassion on them, but not before all the hatred and damage they have done to God's image within them have been repaired. They have to be taught how to love, something which they have never learned in their lifetime, and how to be compassionate, and to show care for others. This process, in your language, takes a long time. When they have learned to live all over again and have asked forgiveness of each one they have hurt or destroyed, then my Father shows them mercy. I am not saying that everyone repents like that."

"So, some go to hell?" the boy continued.

"I did not say that."

"There is a hell, and if a person dies unrepentant, that means that that person has chosen not to love God. God will not force a person to live with Him, if he or she does not want to. So, there has to be a place where people go who have chosen not to love and even at the end refuse to love. This is a place where all the loveless, and totally selfish people go. Can you imagine living forever with totally selfish people who care nothing for you, and who will never love you? That is hell. My Father sends no one there. People choose not to be with those who love, because they can't stand the sight of goodness. Hell is the other option, where goodness has long been abandoned."

"Is the world coming to an end soon?" another boy blurted out.

"No, don't waste time worrying about it. My Father will not bring the world to an end until His creation is first brought to perfection in His Son. That will take a long, long time. The last day of your own life is the only end of the world you have to be concerned about.

"Remember, my Father created you to be happy, and to enjoy the life He gave you. Loving your Father in heaven and showing compassion to others on earth is not only the key to heaven, it is the key to happiness and peace here on earth. Your wonderful teacher has been training you in many ways how you can do that. Listen to him. He is a good teacher, and a good man."

The whole class clapped their appreciation to him for coming to visit them.

"Thank you, Joshua," Earl said, as he hugged him.

All the students then surrounded Joshua and asked if he minded being hugged.

"No, not at all. I love it. You don't know how much I wished people loved me."

They were all crying as they walked out of the room to their next class, crying because Joshua had to leave them. They had never known anyone who showed them such love, not in what he did or said, but in the way he looked at them and without words told each one he loved them, and with a love they had never known before. And to think they would never see him again.

As they were leaving the room, Joshua, knowing their feelings, called them and said out loud so all could hear him, "Don't feel sad. I will see you again, and remember, I am always with you, especially when you gather together in my name and walk up to receive me into your hearts."

As the students left, Earl turned to Joshua and said, "I will never be able to thank you enough for what you have done. I know you have changed these students' lives."

"It is not that simple, Earl. They are going to have to go through tough times before they come home. And they will make mistakes. Look at Peter. He was with me day and night for three years and still could make a mess of things, so don't think you're going to have a class full of angels. It doesn't work that way."

Earl's next class was coming into the room, so Earl walked Joshua to the office and said good-bye. As Joshua left, Earl could not control the pain of loneliness he felt. For the first time he understood the pain the apostles must have felt when Jesus left them. He went to the teachers' room and for a few minutes wept, but could explain to no one why he was weeping. Who would understand?

FOR SOME REASON, which was to become clearer as the weeks passed, Joshua was moving farther and farther west. Texas was not far from Louisiana, and the weather there was much more to Joshua's liking. He was in a border town, and the people were for the most part Spanish speaking. Not far from the edge of town was a high chain-link fence topped with razor wire to keep out unwanted aliens from across the border. Immigration police were everywhere. A patrol vehicle wandered along the dirt road that ran for miles along the border.

A balding, heavyset man in gray trousers and red suspenders came lumbering out of the nearby café, and walked toward an old model Chevy station wagon. Taking out an oversized red handkerchief, he looked around, wiped his brow, waved to a group of immigration police standing nearby, and wiggled his way into the car, then rolled the window down and sat there.

Joshua was sitting on a bench at one of the storefronts. He had been watching the man since he drove up an hour or so before. The man in the car noticed him looking at him, and waved a friendly "hello." Joshua got up and walked over to the station wagon.

"My name's Joshua," he said as he extended his hand.

"Pleased to meet you," he said. "My name's Richard, Richard Sinner."

Joshua laughed. "You don't look like a sinner."

"But I really am. I have a birth certificate and baptismal record to prove it. I am not just an ordinary sinner. I am a wild sinner besides."

"How do you figure that?"

"Well, my mother's maiden name was Wild, so when my father and mother married, the newspaper announced, 'Wild-Sinner Married,' so, I've been a Wild Sinner all my life."

"Are you a farmer? You dress like a farmer."

"I guess we all are up our way. I'm a priest."

"This is your parish?"

"No, my parish is in North Dakota."

"What are you doing way down here?"

"I come down here all the time."

"What for?"

"To pick up the poor people coming across the border."

"How do you do it? The place is saturated with police."

"I just sit here in my car and wait."

"Wait for what?"

"I wait until the police go to lunch. Then, when they go to lunch, the people on the other side of the fence come out of hiding, lift up the fence, and crawl through. I pack them in the car and take off."

"Where do you go?"

"We drive to the Canadian border, where I drop them off with people who are waiting for them to find jobs for them. The Canadian government is much more humane in their treatment of these people."

"How many have you taken up there?"

"Over the past six or seven years about two thousand."

"Did you ever get arrested?"

"Oh yes, a number of times. Then, the next day there's a big spread in the newspaper, 'Governor Sinner's Brother Arrested Again.'"

"Does he get upset?"

"No, he just tells the reporters, 'Well, that's my brother. I know, I'm not going to change him. He's a good priest and I love him, and I respect him.'"

Joshua laughed, and it was a deep rolling belly laugh. It was easy to tell Joshua liked the man.

"You know, Richard, you and St. Peter would have been the best of friends. He would be the type to do things like that."

"Where are you from, young man?"

"I just came over from New Orleans."

"What are you doing here?"

"I wanted to meet you for one thing. I had heard a lot about this modern-day Good Samaritan who was helping all these people to find a better life for themselves and their families. You are a good man for a Wild Sinner."

The priest chuckled. He was a gentle, simple man, with no pretense, no sham, and with a heart as big as his person.

"You are a good priest, Richard. I wish I had more priests like you, good shepherds, wandering around and gathering up the lost and hurting sheep. There are so many sheep lost in the wilderness these days, and few are willing to go out and look for them and bring them home. My heart breaks when I see these people trying so desperately to find a new life for themselves. They are a people who never abandon hope. They risk life and all they have to make a better living for their families.

"America is like heaven to them. They try so hard to enter this land of hope and promise, while others lock the gates to keep them out. What do you think it will be like when they arrive at the gates of heaven? Which of them will God be happy to welcome home? Do you think He will say to some, 'There is no room'?"

"I never looked at it that way. But that is going to be an interesting time. I would like to be there to witness it."

"You will witness it and all your good deeds will be vindicated. Whatever you have done for the least of my brothers and sisters you have done for me. You have chosen the right path, Richard. May you be blessed, and may all the sheep in your widely spread flock be blessed as well."

"Thank you, young man. You are sort of special yourself, I can tell. And I appreciate your encouragement."

Joshua walked away. The priest followed him with his

eyes, wondering what kind of man he was. "I felt a warmth and a glow inside as he was speaking," the priest thought. "And it seems that he knows the apostles intimately. He promised I would one day witness the judgment and see the outcome of my work. How would he know all these things? He's obviously very stable and balanced, but he knows things that others don't know. How did he know about me, and about me being here right at this moment."

As he watched Joshua, little Mexican-American children walked over to him as if they knew him, just like the children in the gospel stories. Joshua sat down on a rocky ledge surrounding a water fountain, and began telling stories to them. As they sat there enthralled, Richard's mind scanned the gospel stories, and then he knew. His eyes filled with tears, and he knew also that his work was good and that it was blessed, and that he was not odd as many thought him to be for doing this kind of work.

Joshua did not stay long at the border. There was little he could do there. He was anxious to visit another place before he went further toward the coast. It was a university in Waco. Baptist and fundamentalist, it had taken a bold step in trying to be faithful to Jesus' prayer for unity. The president of the university, under a directive from the board of trustees, called in the Catholic and Baptist chaplains, and told them that in the future, the board would like them to work together as a team. This, the board felt, was a way the university could be responsive to the prayer of Jesus at the Last Supper, the prayer that his disciples would all be one. So, rather than doing everything separately, from now on the Christian family there would work as one family in Christ, showing a unity of purpose and love among the Christian faculty and students.

At the time it was announced, both chaplains were astounded at such a forward-looking decision, as it had been a strictly Baptist-oriented university. Both chaplains were thrilled that they could now work and plan together, knowing that it was the accepted policy of the institution.

When Joshua arrived at the campus, it was late in the afternoon. It was a beautiful spring day, not too hot, and the best time of the year in Texas. Spring flowers were blooming, and the air was clean and fresh. Wandering through the campus, he talked to students as he met them along the paths. Some were friendly and some were quite aloof, having not the slightest idea who this stranger was.

Walking along, he noticed a bulletin board listing current events. One of the notices announced an ecumenical religious service scheduled to be held at the chapel that evening. All students were welcome. Joshua asked the students if the services were open to the public. No one ever checks, he was told, so they supposed anyone could go.

Joshua took a seat in back of the chapel. By seven o'clock the chapel was almost filled. Strains of Bach and Telemann created a prayerful atmosphere, as people readied themselves for the thought-provoking and prayful evening ahead. Joshua sat there and admired the construction of the chapel. Though unlike Catholic churches with the warmth of saintly memories in mural and statue, the chapel had a quiet, reverential atmosphere that prepared people for prayer.

Though the service was scheduled for seven, people

were still coming, so the clergy waited until everyone was seated. It must have been well promoted, as the crowd was fast exceeding capacity.

Finally, the program began. The president of the university appeared at the podium, and clearly delighted with the turnout, welcomed everyone to the event, the first of its kind on the campus. He then introduced the chaplains and told the congregation how pleased the university was that the chaplains worked so well together, and that the program that evening was the product of their joint venture. The choir was ecumenical and the people in the sanctuary were from different denominations.

The ceremony was a combined prayer service with prayers, music, readings from scripture and the writings of the early Fathers of the Church, converts of the apostles themselves or their disciples, a joint profession of faith that the various chaplains had worked on. Music was a big part of the program so it was a joyful expression of faith. The unique aspect of the service was that it was focused on Jesus. The people really had the feeling that it was not just another scripture service, but that it was more to welcome Jesus into their midst as they opened their hearts to him and asked him for guidance and grace to work together as one family.

Joshua was deeply moved, not just by the ceremony but by the sincerity of the participants who had taken a bold step in response to Jesus' prayer for unity. He knew it would not be easy for them in the days ahead. Reactionaries would make life miserable in an attempt to bring things back where they used to be, armed camps, hostile and competing with one another. While they prayed, he listened and answered their prayers. They had not the slightest idea that he was so close to them that evening, and such an intimate part of their program. Yet, he is always that close when we reach out to him.

As the people left the ceremony afterward, their happy, friendly spirit delighted Joshua. People went out of their way to speak to others whom they did not even know. Many strangers became friends that evening.

Joshua would have liked to speak to those who planned the program and those who allowed it to happen, but he felt they had already done well enough on their own, and were off to a good start, so he thought it best to move on.

The weather was beautiful that evening. Joshua walked around the campus and after a while sat down under a tree and fell asleep. The next morning he woke up to the singing of the birds and was thrilled by the gorgeous sunrise at the east side of the beautiful campus.

After watching the rising sun, and enjoying the sounds of the birds singing, he walked to the cafeteria and got on line with the students. Carrying his tray toward the tables, a group of oriental students told him he was welcome to sit at their table. He accepted, then proceeded to speak in their languages, fluently, much to their surprise. After finding out his name was Joshua, one of the students said that he had a friend who had told him about a man he met not long ago who was named Joshua. He was quite a mysterious person, who had the ability to do wonderful things. "You couldn't be that person, could you?" one of the students said jokingly.

"We never really know who a person is when we meet them, do we?" Joshua quipped, with an impish smile.

"You were at the service last night, weren't you?" one of the other students remarked.

"Yes, I enjoyed it very much."

"We went, too. We're Buddhists, but we found the ceremony very exciting. It brought us all so close together. People whom we didn't even know came over and talked to us last night, and made us feel so much at home. It wasn't just an ordinary religious service. I learned a lot about Jesus last night. Rather than just giving people Bibles, they should make Jesus better known to others. I think Jesus has the answers to the problems people face today. No matter what a person's religion, I think everyone could be inspired and helped by his ideas. He is really a beautiful person."

Joshua listened, and then responded in perfect Mandarin Chinese, "You are right, Feijin Zhou, Jesus' message reaches to the very soul of each human being, no matter what his or her nationality or belief. It is because Jesus is the light that comes forth from God, and shares the very life of God. That is what makes him unique and special."

One of the other students said, "When they were talking about Jesus last night, I had the warmest feeling inside of me, a feeling I never had before. I could have listened to those holy men speak of Jesus all night long."

"You know, I had that same feeling," a young girl student said. "I was deeply moved by what I experienced."

As the students had to leave they told Joshua how much they had enjoyed talking with him, especially in Chinese. "By the way," one of them said, "you knew our names and we never told you our names. And you speak our language fluently, and while you were talking to us, I had the same wonderful feeling I had when they were talking about Jesus last night. And when I asked you before if you were that Joshua my friend told me about, you didn't really answer, but I think you are," he said, smiling.

"I am," Joshua said, though they only half believed. They left wondering, and with much to think about and tell the other students.

Joshua left the campus shortly after finishing breakfast, to continue his journey. He was still moving westward.

THERE WAS NOW an urgency in Joshua's determination to push on toward California. Ordinarily, it was difficult, if not impossible to read his thoughts, but when something was pressing heavily upon him it showed in his total focus on the matter. At this particular time he was focused, focused as never before. He always seemed to know beforehand what might occur, but this time it was different. It was as if it was a matter he could do nothing about, but still had to be present.

San Francisco is one of the most colorful cities in the country, even if one of the most congested. Joshua was winding his way through the streets of the business section, trying to find the offices of the *San Francisco Chronicle*. Finally, he came upon Mission Avenue and entering the building asked the receptionist if he could talk to the editor.

"Do you have an appointment?"

"No."

"What is your name?"

"Joshua."

"Your full name."

"That is my full name."

"Hello, sir, there is a man here by the name of Joshua who would like to speak with you."

"About what?"

"Mr. Joshua, what did you want to see the editor about?"

"About something very important that is going to take place in the city within the next few days."

The receptionist relayed the message and the editor told her to send him up.

After going through security, Joshua went to the editor's office.

"Please take a seat, Joshua. How can I help you?"

"I do not want help. I want to share some information with you that is extremely urgent and the people must know about it."

"What is that?"

"Within the next two weeks there is going to be a major earthquake, the massive one that has been predicted for so long. It is about to happen. A major part of the city will shift down the plate and sink beneath the ocean. It will be similar to the earthquake in Alaska many years ago, but the devastation will be far greater. The people must know about it."

"May I ask how you know about this? Are you a geologist or a seismologist?"

"No."

"Well, what is the source of your information?"

What could he say, "I created this world, and I know everything that is taking place in it, even to the tiniest detail?" Hardly.

"If I told you, I know you would not believe me. But I know for a fact that it is about to take place."

"I can't print in the newspaper, 'A man with an uncanny sense of natural phenomena predicts a major earthquake in the San Francisco area within the next few weeks.' They'd laugh me out of town."

"What will you do when it happens and they find out you knew about it beforehand, and refused to print the story? If you do not believe me, call the seismologists, and ask them. They will have slight signs of disturbances already. Or if you won't do that, then, watch the animals in the streets for the next weeks. You will see them acting strangely as they sense the imminent danger."

"I think you had better leave. I'm sorry, sir, but I can't print a story like that."

Joshua got up and walked out.

As he left the building, he thought of going to other newspapers, but decided against it since their reaction would be the same. While walking along, he happened to walk past *China News.* "Chinese people have curious minds," he thought, "and the editor there might be willing to take a chance. But it would be a help if someone could introduce me."

Joshua did have Chinese friends who lived in the area and who could possibly vouch for him. Their names were

Harry, Alice, and Andrew Lam. Harry was a research scientist and a man of impeccable character. Joshua contacted him. They met for lunch, and when Harry heard what Joshua had to say, he couldn't help wonder, as a scientist, why seismologists had no evidence of movement of the plates. However, his respect for Joshua's intelligence and prudence was sufficient enough to convince him that some catastrophe was about to happen. Whether Joshua was right in every detail was not important, but Harry was convinced that some disaster of frightening proportions was about to occur. The first thought that came to his mind was the earthquake insurance on his house, because he knew there would be no way he could sell his house within the brief period of time before the tragedy was expected to occur.

Harry agreed to introduce Joshua to the editor of the *China Times* with whom he was friendly, though the man was not a close friend. Harry phoned the editor and told him about Joshua, and of his high opinion of him, and asked if Joshua could stop in to visit with him. The man agreed, so Joshua met with him later in the afternoon.

As he entered the office, the editor welcomed him cordially. To the editor's surprise, Joshua spoke to him in perfect Chinese.

"Your name is Joshua."

"Yes, and your name is Mr. Chang."

"Yes," the man chuckled in surprise. "I presume Mr. Lam told you my name?"

"No."

"Interesting. I was talking with my son last night. He mentioned to me that he met a man named Joshua, a rather strange man, who impressed him with his great wisdom and understanding. He also told me this Joshua spoke fluent Chinese and that this Joshua knew his name without having been introduced to him. You wouldn't be that same man, would you?"

"Your son attends the university in Waco?"

"Yes."

"Yes, I am that same Joshua."

"My son was very impressed with you. He wished he could have spent more time with you."

"Your son is a very perceptive young man. He has a searching mind. Perhaps someday we may meet again."

"Now, Joshua, what is it you wanted to share with me?"

"I realize that I cannot offer you any scientific evidence to support what I wish to share with you, but it is very important that you believe me. Millions of lives are at stake. Within the next two weeks, an earthquake of gigantic proportions will occur. This whole area will slide off into the bay. The city will sink to the bottom of the bay, and the whole population will be destroyed unless they leave the city and flee up into the hills. I know you have a difficult time believing this, especially from a stranger you have never met and never heard of except from your son. You may contact seismologists and ask them if they have seen any movement along the fault lines. They will tell you that there has been minor evidence of movement, but nothing to worry about.

"Then ask them if this movement has been continuous over a period of time. They will tell you that it has been. That is all they will be able to tell you, because it is too early.

By the time they have more conclusive evidence it will be too late. That is why I am telling this to you now."

"Joshua, I don't know how to respond. I respect you because of what little I have heard about you within the past few hours, but a story like this, with unsupported evidence, is very risky for a newspaper to print. If it is not true, and people act on it, we would lose all credibility. I promise, however, that I will contact a number of seismologists and ask them for information. If what they tell me agrees with what you have told me, we will consider the evidence and, together with the publisher and staff, we will make our decision. That is the most I can do."

"I have confidence in your sincerity, Mr. Chang. I know when you publish the story, you will save many lives."

"Thank you, Joshua. I do appreciate your coming here and sharing your concern with our newspaper. I promise to weigh the matter conscientiously."

The two men shook hands, and Joshua left. The editor watched him intently as he went, wondering what kind of man this was who had such insight and such wisdom, and could even predict natural calamities.

During the course of the next week Joshua visited many of the churches, asking if he could talk to the pastors and assistants. Many did not have the time to meet with him; the secretaries told him he should make an appointment. Others thought he was a crackpot, and sent him on his way. A few clergy who were heavy into the conviction that the end of the world was imminent, listened to him, and thought his message would be interesting material for their next Sunday's sermon, though they really did not believe it with any urgency.

One humble priest who was considered strange by other clergy because he dressed in the same clothes as the poor and sometimes slept with the homeless in the parks and on the streets could see in Joshua something beneath his appearance. The priest's insight, which came from deep faith, conditioned by lifelong pain and rejection and disillusionment with the artificial values of so much of society, glimpsed for a fleeting moment the true identity of this simple wanderer. He was accustomed to seeing goodness and even nobility of character among the poor and homeless. To others they might be ne'er-do-wells, and beggars, or misfits. To this humble priest, they were the tragic, lonely outcasts of society, dearer to God than the many who basked in the deluded vision of their own righteousness, and social propriety. They at least, in their emptiness, had room in their hearts for Someone other than themselves.

Joshua met this priest one morning as he went into a café for breakfast. The priest was sitting in a booth, drinking a cup of coffee and reading a newspaper.

"May I sit with you, Father?"

The man laughed. "You call me Father. I guess everyone knows me with my ambiguous reputation."

"No, I know you because I can see you are a priest," Joshua said with insistence. "You are a rare good shepherd, in the best meaning of the word."

"How do you know I am a priest?"

"I can see the mark on your soul, the mark of your priesthood. You have preserved it intact and unblemished."

Tears welled up in the bloodshot eyes of the unkempt priest, and began to course down his cheeks.

"You can see my priesthood beneath these rags I am wearing, and my unshaven face?"

"Yes, it shines like a brilliant light through all the holes in your clothes."

"Can I buy you a cup of coffee . . . Now I don't even know your name."

"Joshua."

"Joshua, Jesus. It means Jesus in Hebrew, you know."

"Yes, I know."

"My name is Jim. I suppose he would be much like you if he were here today, seeing into people's hearts and saying things to people like you said to me. I think about him a lot. I have nothing else to do anymore. I try to be his presence to these poor people."

"That is why I am here. You have brought these people my presence, now I want you to bring them my message."

The priest looked at Joshua in shock.

"You mean to tell me . . . ? But if you are who you say you are, why would you come to me?"

"I have something very important for you to do."

"Look at me! What could I do for you? I have no standing in the community. Who would listen to me? The only ones who respect me are the homeless, and that is only because they know I care for them."

"They are the ones I want you to speak to."

Then, realizing he had forgotten to order Joshua's coffee, he said, "Oh, I almost forgot . . . Waiter, would you bring a cup of coffee for my friend.

"I'm sorry for the interruption. You want me to speak to the homeless. About what?"

"About something very important. In a very short time, there is going to be a massive earthquake, the one everyone fears, but for which no one is prepared. I come to you because you are a humble man, and your faith opens your heart to listen."

Joshua, knowing the priest found it difficult to believe that God would visit him, began to talk to him in Hebrew. The priest was shocked.

"You speak Hebrew perfectly. It is Aramaic Hebrew. Where did you learn it? How did you know I knew Hebrew?"

"I learned it as a child. I know you taught scripture and Hebrew in the seminary. I knew if I spoke in Hebrew, you would be impressed."

"I am impressed. Tell me your message and I will listen with an open heart."

"I want you to pass the word around among your homeless friends that they are very important to God, and He does not want anything to happen to them. Then tell them that in a short time a powerful earthquake will rock the valley and the city will slide off into the bay. Tell them they are to go up into the hills and stay far away from the city. God does not want anything to happen to them, they are important to God. Go, give them that message. They will listen to you. They love you. You are their shepherd and like me you came down and were not ashamed to be one of them."

"When is this earthquake supposed to take place?"

"Within the next two weeks. So, it is important that you

spread the message, and have your people spread the message. Those who listen to them will be saved; those who laugh at them in disbelief will be lost. Now go and spread the word among them."

Reluctantly, and feeling rather foolish because it was so foreign to his highly trained and scholarly background, the priest paid the bill, and left to spread the message.

Word spread rapidly. Evangelicals and fundamentalists were more open to listen, because many of them were expecting that the end might be imminent. The more sophisticated and overeducated scoffed at the idea. "Certainly, if there was any danger of an earthquake, the scientists would have given us advance warning," was the most common reaction.

The newspapers, however, did pick up the story. Strange, they wouldn't listen to Joshua, but they were intrigued by the army of homeless beggars as they called them, under the guidance of a strange priest, wandering the streets warning people of the imminence of a major earthquake. The *China News* also checked on what Joshua had told them, and it was true, the seismologists were receiving faint signals of geologic disturbances. And it was also true that the disturbances did seem to be increasing, but there was no indication that anything catastrophic was about to occur. So, no warning was issued. The *China News* decided to publish the story as a public service, but included the scientists' findings as well, so the people themselves would have a chance to make up their own minds, and have time to prepare for whatever eventualities might occur.

There were some who took the news stories seriously,

and listened to the warnings of the homeless people. There was no run on real estate agents to quickly sell homes. What many did decide to do was take vacations early, or go and visit relatives for the next few weeks, because that was a time frame within which the catastrophe was supposed to take place.

Father Jim delivered Joshua's message to other priests, as well as to clergy of other denominations and religions. Some who knew him from the old days and were aware of his brilliant mind took him seriously and told their people at services the following weekend. These clergy told their congregations that even though there was no scientific evidence as yet, there seemed to be enough reason for the populace to take precautions. Often when information on such matters from the scientists is forthcoming, it is too late for officials to set up a command headquarters to mobilize the population and organize a strategy for the safe and orderly evacuation of all the people.

After informing the clergy, Father Jim personally told as many people as he could. He contacted his relatives and friends. Some were appreciative, some were skeptical. One of his friends, a Jewish man named Peter, knew Joshua very well, and in fact was very close to him. He had no trouble believing the priest, though he was deeply disturbed at the possibility of such a tragedy. Immediately after Father Jim's warning, he told his office staff, and strongly suggested they leave town for the next few weeks. He himself took a flight to New York to conduct business from his New York office until the situation passed.

News of the possibility of an earthquake created pandemonium among many people. Government offices were deluged with phone calls. The governor and mayor were furious that information about the possibility of an earthquake was publicized without any scientific data to back it up, and without any permission from their offices. They sent out instructions to all the relevant departments to inform the people that there was no need to worry about an earthquake. There was no scientific evidence whatever to warrant such fears.

In the meantime, an official from the archdiocesan chancery office called in Father Jim and severely reprimanded him for his gross imprudence in using the homeless in such a cynical way, knowing there was no solid information concerning any impending catastrophe. The official demanded that he publicly retract the warning about an earthquake.

"I cannot," he told the official.

"What do you mean, you cannot?"

"I know there is going to be an earthquake of major proportions, and I have an obligation in conscience to warn the people."

"How do you know there is going to be an earthquake? The scientists deny it."

"I don't care what the scientists say. By the time they have enough data, it will be too late to mobilize the government agencies to plan an orderly evacuation of the city."

"I think you must be losing it, Jim. You used to have such a good reputation. Everybody in the archdiocese used to admire you for your brilliance. Why are you doing such crazy things? You are embarrassing the archbishop and the whole archdiocese."

"What do I tell him?" Father Jim said to himself. "Do I tell him that God came to me and told me to do it? He would really think I'm mad."

The priest had no way of defending himself. He would just have to endure the anger and the ridicule, and stand firm in his conviction. He realized for the first time how prophets felt when religious leaders demanded that they retract prophecies that disturbed the people.

There was a long silence. Then, the official slowly and in measured tone told the priest that if he did not retract his prophecy, he would be suspended from the functions of his priesthood.

Father Jim just looked at him, and for a moment said nothing, though a tear appeared in the corner of his eye. "St. Thomas Aquinas once wrote," he said, "that if, after thoroughly investigating an issue, a person believed in his heart something to be true, and was asked to deny it, he should be willing to endure even excommunication rather than violate his conscience, and deny what he believed to be true. Is that what you are asking me to do?"

The priest blushed. "This meeting is ended, Jim," were his last words. And he walked out in anger, leaving Father Jim sitting in the room by himself.

When Father Jim left the chancery, he was despondent. Working with the homeless depressed him. It was not easy, being so different from life on a college campus. This confrontation with Church officials, whom he knew in his heart were trying to do God's work, deepened that depression. All priests hope their superiors will understand and appreciate the work they do, especially when their ministries are difficult ones. To be not only misunderstood but to be reprimanded and stripped of your priesthood for fidelity to a special calling is more painful than one can imagine.

As Father Jim walked down the street, people who knew him, and mostly everybody in the city knew him, did not even greet him. Some made cutting remarks as they walked past. Others sneered. The priest just looked and smiled. He must have been a sorry sight—his hair, not recently cut, and almost totally gray, as he was no longer a young man; his shoes with holes in them; his clothes, just like other homeless people's clothes, charitable people's castaways; walking with a slight limp as his arthritis was aggravated by daily exposure to the elements. So different was this from just a few years before, when as a major seminary professor, proud of his reputation as a scholar, and noted for his impeccable taste for fine dress and his remarkable talent for polite conversation, he was invited to the homes of the wealthy and the powerful.

As he walked along, he was surprised to see Joshua approaching him.

"I never expected to bump into you down in this neighborhood," the priest said to Joshua.

"I know how difficult it has been for you to carry this burden. Do not be afraid! I am with you, and by your side no matter what happens. I was there in the office with you as you were shamed and humbled. You carried yourself well. You proved yourself to be the bigger person than your accuser. I am proud of you."

"Thank you, Joshua. I am becoming more and more convinced that you are who you say you are. I also feel more convinced of the urgency of the mission you entrusted to me. I will stay on course. I expect nothing from them; I need nothing from them, so I am not afraid. And I love my priesthood. They cannot take it away from me and I will never lay it aside."

"You were never more a priest than you are now, Jim, a true good shepherd, sacrificing everything to save the flock. And you have made the crippled sheep little shepherds to spread the message and save others. I am proud of what they are doing. They will save many people's lives. I am grateful to you, Jim, for guiding them through this difficult mission."

"Joshua, one thing I wanted to ask you."

"What is that?"

"Is this the end of the world?"

"This earthquake has been long in coming. People were warned about it over and over, and yet they still hesitate to leave this area. This is not the end of the world, nor is it the beginning of the end of the world. These natural disasters have always occurred and will continue to occur as the planet evolves. It has nothing to do with the ending of the world. The world will not end until the process of creation arrives at the perfection my Father intended for it. All things must first be gathered into His Son, and become one in him before he offers all creation to his Father. Just look around you! What do you see? Do you see a world that is united in God's Son? No, the end is a long way off."

CHAPTER 17

AS THE DAYS went on, the homeless fanned out through every part of the city, trying to convince people of the imminence of the earthquake. At one point, Father Jim was contacted by a priest friend who asked if he would offer Mass at his parish, as he had to be out of town. Father Jim was delighted, as he had not offered Mass in church in a long time. He had been having Eucharistic celebrations for the homeless in abandoned warehouses, and in open fields, never asking what religion they belonged to. It would have been ridiculous. All they knew was they had a priest who cared for them and they wanted to be part of whatever he was. He belonged to Jesus. They wanted to belong to Jesus. It was that simple. So, knowing how this would please Jesus, he looked upon them all as one family, Jesus' family. When they came to receive Communion, he had no problem with that.

The church where Father Jim was asked to offer Mass was in an old part of town. When word circulated, the homeless came from all over. Joshua also came. The church was filled way beyond capacity. It was a motley crowd, an unusual parish. There were people of every possible description; besides the homeless who were obvious, there was a large assortment of Orientals, Chinese, Japanese, Filipinos, Vietnamese. There were African-Americans, Native Americans, Americans of every other description. There were poor people, middle-class people, well-to-do people. The composition of the parish reflected the spirit of the pastor, who had a compassionate, Christ-like heart that made everyone feel welcome. Whatever he believed, they believed. In his sermons he taught them all that Jesus taught, and they believed. Baptism was like in the early days, simple: "Do you believe all that I have been teaching you?"

"Yes, I do."

"Then, I baptize you," etc.

When they came up to receive Communion, he gave them Jesus. They were all part of Jesus' family.

The people warmly welcomed Father Jim when he arrived. Unfortunately, he was not feeling well. He had a bad cough and looked very weak, probably because he had eaten practically nothing in the last few days.

As soon as he started Mass, he noticed Joshua sitting in the front pew, watching and listening intently.

"My sisters and brothers, we come before God with humble hearts. We recognize our weakness, our sinfulness before God. We know you understand us because you made us, but we still ask your forgiveness. Lord, have mercy."

"Lord, have mercy."

"Christ, have mercy."

"Lord, have mercy."

The Mass progressed smoothly. The sermon was short, very simple. Father Jim's weakness was becoming more noticeable. "My friends," he started out, "I enjoy so much offering Mass with you, because as I look around, I see a genuine Christian community, a family of caring people, a gathering that would please the heart of the Christ. I can see by the look on his face that he is pleased. (The priest had a sly grin as he said it. Joshua lowered his head, hoping he would not betray his presence.) In the days ahead that spirit is going to be more important than ever before in your lives. The message that has been circulating for the past week is coming closer to reality each day. Seismologists are noticing increasing evidence of greater movement along the fault lines, and I urge you to heed the warning. Do not stay in the city any longer. This whole section of the city will not be here two weeks from now, indeed, even before that. So, do not delay. Do not wait until what you think will be the last minute. It may very well happen in the middle of the night.

"People ask how I know. I have been reluctant to say before, but I will tell you all now. I know what is taking place because, because, . . . I have been privileged to have been told by God, by Jesus. At first, I did not believe him. I did not believe it was Jesus, but then he proved it in ways I could not doubt. You know I have always been a careful, prudent man, not prone to rashness or impetuous actions. I would not be saying these things now if I was not totally convinced of the authenticity of this message. Please, do not tarry any longer in this city.

"I was asked by people if this earthquake was a punishment from God, because of all the evil in the city, because it is an abomination before God. I asked Jesus about this and he told me that this city is no different from any other city, but that this earthquake had been predicted by scientists for years, and no one listens. This occurrence is just an expected natural phenomenon. And he became angry at the self-righteous and hypocritical judgment that called the people here evil. The people here are good people. There are some who choose to do evil things that hurt others, but they are few compared to the vast number of good people. People have different kinds of weaknesses, different kinds of sins, but all are struggling as best they can to do what is right. No one should look down on others because of their inclinations and weaknesses. That is what is really offensive to God. My Father understands the weaknesses of every individual, and judges each one with understanding and compassion. No, this tragedy is not a punishment from God. It is merely a natural occurrence. That is what Jesus told me, and I relay it to you."

The priest continued the Mass. At Communion time, as he held up the Consecrated Bread, and was saying the words, "Behold the Lamb of God who takes away the sins of the world," his face turned white. Placing the sacred vessel on the altar, he began to sway and then collapsed and fell to the floor.

Joshua calmly walked up to the altar. His sense of presence and authority caused the Eucharistic ministers and others standing around to allow him to take charge. Lifting up the limp body of the priest, he carried him to the side of the sanctuary and settled him into the large wood-carved armchair. Resting his hand on his head, he prayed. The priest opened his eyes, and looked up, bewildered. Joshua told him to stay seated; he would take care of everything. Then, walking back to the head of the aisle, he stopped at the front pew and asked one of the homeless women kneeling there to come up to the altar. She was a striking woman, not noticeably pretty, but a woman of dignity, by the name of Sophie. Her clothes were old, but neat. One could easily tell that, though she had nothing, she kept herself well.

Leading her up to the altar, Joshua told her to stand with the other Eucharistic ministers. He then gave them Communion. When he finished, he gave them the sacred vessels so they could distribute Communion to the people. When he placed the sacred vessel in the woman's hands, he told her to give out Communion in the center aisle in Father Jim's place.

At first people were reluctant to receive Communion from her. The first one to come up in her line was a little homeless girl about nine years old. When the others saw that, they felt ashamed and people began to form in her line.

While they were distributing Communion, Joshua sat next to Father Jim, who was by now fully recuperated. "Joshua, if I didn't know better, I would have thought you did this to me just so you could have that homeless woman distribute Communion."

Joshua smiled.

When Communion was finished, Joshua told the woman

to bring Communion to Father Jim. Offered him the Body and Blood of Christ, he consumed it and gave the chalice back to her. Leading her to the altar, Joshua asked her to read the closing prayers. When she finished, Joshua gave the blessing and together with Father Jim, the three processed down the aisle to the back of the church where they greeted the people as they left.

As the people were leaving the church, a loud rumble shook the building violently. Windows shattered, a life-size statue tumbled from its pedestal and came crashing to the marble floor. Chunks of plaster shook loose and fell on the pews. Pandemonium broke out immediately. People started screaming, and ran out of the building as quickly as they could, almost trampling one another as they forced their way through the doors.

The tremor lasted for only a few seconds, just long enough to convince everyone that Father Jim's prophecy was accurate. Something was happening, and as in other earthquakes, more violent tremors followed smaller ones. The people scattered in all directions in a frantic attempt to rush home and pick up their families, and as much of their belongings as they could, and leave the city before the cars and trucks bound up the city in total gridlock.

Joshua and Father Jim led the homeless who had come to the Mass, up from the center of the city to the outskirts. It was almost two and a half hours before they reached a safe area. Along the way they met other homeless people. They passed the word on to them that this was the time to leave the city, and that they should tell the others as they met them. Through their remarkable network they were able to reach most of the homeless in the city. The rest would see the others walking in large numbers on their way out of the city, and would join them. By late afternoon, practically all the homeless had left town. Joshua was with Father Jim and a large group of homeless. At one point, Joshua turned and looked across the sinking city. He sat down, and with his head in his hands began to cry. "Why, why, why did you not listen? I tried so hard to reach out to you, to warn you. You laughed, you would not listen, you would not believe. Now you are no more."

Though the homeless had reached safety, the rest of the people who tried to leave in cars were soon trapped in the gridlock. Reluctant to abandon their precious vehicles, many just sat in them hoping that, through some miracle, the gridlock would end and they could continue out of the city. That would not happen.

At about six o'clock, the second tremor occurred. It was 4.5 on the Richter scale. By that time people were trapped. There was no way to leave the city, except on foot. Not only the streets but the sidewalks as well were in gridlock from the rush of people running in all directions.

An hour later, the big one came. It was 8.0 on the Richter scale. The whole city shook violently. Water mains cracked open and geysers sprayed water in all directions. The streets were filling with water. People were slipping and falling, while others trampled them underfoot. Humanity lost all veneer of civility, and became like a herd of animals running in panic from a fire, trampling one another in the confusion. Old buildings collapsed. As the earth shifted, it soon began to slide, and tilt, which forced tall buildings to crack in half and come tumbling down upon the screaming crowds beneath. No one had ever experienced a quake like this one. Usually the earth would shake for a few seconds and cause perhaps severe damage, but this time the earth did not stop moving. The waterfront began to slide into the bay. Gradually the water rose higher and higher as the city slid farther into the water. In the distance one could see the Golden Gate Bridge collapse. Everywhere there was chaos. People trying to escape were slipping and sliding. The bay was a teeming mass of bodies, moving frantically in an attempt to find chunks of wood or Styrofoam to cling to for safety.

As the city continued to slide, it was not long before the center of the city and the business section had become the waterfront. But not for long, as the skyscrapers slowly slid under the water. With such a large portion of the city now under water, the momentum built up, and the sliding accelerated. Soon the electricity shut down, as utility officials realized what was happening and turned off all the electricity in the city to prevent people from being electrocuted in the rivers that flowed through the streets.

In a few hours it was dark. Screams and sirens filled the darkness far into the night. It was the most chilling experience a human being could imagine. In all of nature there was nothing that could compare to this cataclysmic horror.

By morning all was quiet. People who had managed to reach the outskirts of the city looked out in shock and disbelief. There was nothing there. Where there had been just a few hours before a thriving, throbbing metropolis, now there was nothing, just water. San Francisco was no more.

The survivors could not enjoy their freedom. They were dev-astated, shaken to their very souls. They had escaped from the jaws of death and were still alive to tell it. But the trauma was almost as bad, perhaps worse than death. The dead were free now in another world, hopefully a world of peace with God and loved ones. But the survivors would live on with the memory and the nightmare of what happened last night.

Emergency crews were picking up the survivors, bring-ing them to shelters where they could at least lie down, if not sleep. Many could not even lie down, afraid to go to sleep. The nightmare was too vivid. They just talked to each other to distract themselves from the sadness and the depression that overwhelmed their souls. Talking was the only way they could process their agony and preserve their sanity. Some did lose their minds and wandered aimlessly. Though no one knew him, Joshua wandered through the crowds and the shelters bringing comfort and healing and hope everywhere he went.

CHAPTER 18

THE SHOCK OF the earthquake swept across the nation, and, indeed, the whole world. As the chaos gradually cleared, attention eventually focused on Father Jim and the homeless people who were the heroes of the tragedy. As San Francisco no longer existed, there were no news agencies from there to cover the story. Media people came from neighboring cities and from far away, trying to track down Father Jim and the key homeless people who were responsible for spreading the prophecy.

After searching, the various reporters finally found the priest. He was gracious to them when they wanted an interview. He considered it an important part of his ministry, to spread messages he knew Joshua wanted him to disseminate.

One day a television crew from CNN tracked him down and asked if they could interview him for a nationwide television special that would be aired within the next few days. He consented.

"Father, how did you know there was going to be an earthquake?" the reporter asked.

"I will be very frank," the priest replied, "though no one will probably believe me. One day, while having breakfast, a stranger entered the restaurant and came over to the table where I was sitting. He knew my name. He asked if he could speak with me. I told him yes and he sat down.

"He then began to speak in Aramaic, not Hebrew, mind you, but Aramaic, an ancient Hebrew dialect no longer spoken, a language I could understand from my scripture background. In time I became completely convinced that the person I was speaking to was none other than Jesus himself. I was naturally shocked."

"How could you be sure it was Jesus?" the reporter asked.

"Well, at that point I wasn't totally convinced but very impressed. Later that day I was convinced when two homeless people told me that as they were walking down the street approaching the café where I was eating breakfast, a man suddenly appeared out of thin air in front of the café and proceeded to walk inside. They watched him as he walked directly to my table. When they told me that I knew then for certain.

"To get back to the café. I asked him what he wanted with me, as I was no one of importance. He then proceeded to tell me that he had a message for me to deliver. He told me about the earthquake that he said was imminent. I had a hard time accepting it, as seismologists had said nothing about any movement of the geologic plates in the area. But realizing who it was who was telling me, I knew it must be right, so I agreed to follow his instructions. He told me that I should inform the homeless and have them deliver the message throughout the city, as there was no other way of doing it, since people would not believe it.

"I gathered a group around me and told them the prophecy. Because they respected me, they believed me, and followed the instructions I gave them. They told their friends and passed the word around among the homeless population, who in turn spread the message throughout the community at large. Most ignored them, some believed. Officials were angry."

"What about the churches? Didn't you share the prophecy with your religious superiors?" the reporter asked.

"I shared them with individual pastors. Most were kind toward me but did not believe what I told them. I knew I would get the same response from the chancery. When eventually I did discuss the matter with one of the officials, the response was not pleasant. But I have no bad feelings toward them. I pray for them, and I feel sorry for them now, as they are no longer with us."

"Father Jim, this man whom you identify as Jesus, do you know where he is now, where we might be able to contact him?"

"No. I have no idea of his whereabouts."

"So many people today are convinced that the world is going to end this year. Did your friend have anything to say about the end of the world being imminent?"

"He did speak about the end of the world," the priest

continued, "but was insistent that the world will not end for a long, long time. He said that the world will come to an end when his Father's creation reaches its perfection, and when all creation is gathered together into God's Son. And he said that from looking around us one can easily tell that that is not about to happen soon."

"People in other parts of the country are saying that this earthquake is a punishment from God for all the evil people that are concentrated in this city, this recent city, I should say. Did this Jesus have anything to say about that?" the reporter asked.

"Yes, he was quite angry with the hypocrisy and self-righteousness of those people who say that. He further said that God is more offended by people's hypocrisy and self-righteousness than by the weaknesses and frailty of those they despise as evil. Then he went on to say something very curious, which I am still thinking about."

"What is that?"

"He said that God has unique work for each human being. Accomplishing that work demands that each person be designed differently with different gifts and different abilities. With these positive gifts there are inevitable weaknesses and limitations, some quite severe, that the person may have to carry as a cross all his life. Others should not judge such people harshly, but be compassionate and leave judgment to God, if they want God to be merciful to them. That was quite a remarkable revelation to me."

"These people with you," the reporter said, "they seem very devoted and protective of you. They are homeless, are they not?"

"Yes, they are my friends. We are all homeless."

"But you are a priest. Don't you have a parish?"

"This is my parish. It is not a canonically established parish. I did have a parish, but I chose this one instead. This is where Jesus wants me to be."

"I have heard of you before," the reporter continued. "Weren't you a scripture professor?"

"Yes, I taught scripture and Semitic languages at a university for years after I got my doctorate at the Angelicum in Rome."

"Isn't this a difficult change for you?"

"Not if I love these people, and I do love them. They are my family. I am the father that many of them never had. We live and die together. There are many around the area. I was going to say, 'the city,' but that is no more, and we are homeless again, in a different way."

"Well, thank you, Father, for your very honest answers to some difficult questions. And I hope you are blessed in your work."

"Each day we are," Father Jim replied. "Thank you, and it was a pleasure meeting you and speaking with you."

The reporter and his photographer left after they had taken pictures of the priest and some of the homeless who were standing nearby.

A short time later the interview was aired on national television. Together with the interview, the program showed dramatic pictures of the earthquake and of the city sinking into the bay. The viewers were spellbound as they watched. Concerning the interview with the priest, some listened and were deeply moved, most were skeptical, thinking him odd, perhaps, like many of the people he hung around with. Many self-styled Bible experts said that Jesus could not come back to earth that way before the time he was scheduled to return according to the Book of Revelation. The whole story they contended was contrary to scripture, and just could not happen.

The world will never know how often and in how many places Jesus does come back to visit those who need his presence. He is never very far from any of us, and if he decides on occasion to make his presence known, who can criticize him or fault him. After all he is God; it is not our prerogative to restrict his freedom to our interpretation of scripture.